# REACHING SOL

I hope you enjoy my little story!

Wes Young

9/4/22

# Reaching Sol

## A NOVEL

## Wes Young

Wes Young Writer

REACHING SOL
A NOVEL
By Wes Young
wesyoungwriter.com

ISBN: 978-0-578-39886-0 Trade Paper
eISBN: 978-0-578-39887-7 eBook

This is a work of fiction. Any names or characters, businesses or places, events or incidents, are fictitious. Any resemblance to actual persons, living or dead, or actual events is purely coincidental.

Cover Photos (Lumber City, GA): Erin NeSmith (Instagram: Erin NeSmith Art)
Graphic Design: Emily Wiegert (backpocketbranding.com)
Clock Sketch: Lainie Partain
Author Headshot: Robin Young
Logo: Image by Canva

First Printing, 2022

*For Sharon (Mema)*

# GLOSSARY

**Auto-Tracc:** *See Tracc.*

**BOD:** A bloodstream-based device mandated by CHRON in the 29th century. They are permanent and irremovable. Ostensibly, their function is transferring money. Alleged side effects include loss of self-knowledge and unknowing adoption of a whole new personality.

***Bulletin, The*:** An announcement platform published exclusively by CHRON.

**CHRON:** "Chronological Headquarters for the Restoration of Normalcy," the governing body that rose to power after the Fracture.

**core-grane:** The prevailing power source in the 23rd and 24th centuries.

**Core Power:** That which lies behind it all and would still exist even if nothing else existed.

**Corston:** A small central-Georgia town founded in 1869.

**Crane:** A restraining device used by CHRON agents.

**drigs:** A form of transportation in the 29th century, used primarily by the lower classes.

***First Principles*:** CHRON Publication #328132. Considered the definitive text on time travel.

**fission-rings:** The prevailing power source in the 22nd century.

**flash:** To speedily cool a hot-cooked meal to just above the freezing point. 29th-century food is always eaten cold.

**Fracture, the:** CHRON's term for the first time-jump, which occurred in the 24th century.

**Free-Tracc:** *See Tracc.*

**GID:** A device that is the only known forerunner of the BODs. GIDs were a failed attempt of the year 2763.

**Gor-Implant:** A bloodstream manipulation process administered to all CHRON agents that allows them to travel time without the side effect of memory loss after 40 days.

**Great Stand, the:** The final decisive battle establishing CHRON's dominion over the inhabited world.

**Greeg:** A $29^{th}$-century city.

**Helt Network:** A dense field of low-orbit satellites.

**Lort:** Addictive, momentarily pleasing, and ingested through the eye.

**Module:** A virtual representation of a person or object not physically present.

**Order, The:** A mysterious group operating in the $29^{th}$ century with a history dating back roughly 3,000 years.

**portion-trace:** The study of the genealogy of food ingested by a person in a given year. This discipline is recognized as one of the three fundamental scholarly pillars of the $29^{th}$ century.

**Proce:** An injection used for treating acute Poitexma, a disease something like violent asthma.

**recovery team:** A specialized unit of three CHRON agents tasked with seeking and recovering (or destroying) Temporal Transport evictees who cause or encounter complications in their new time period.

**Recruit Manual:** CHRON Publication #338272. A text used in the training of CHRON agents.

**Rupture, The:** A scientific book written by K. C. Sewell of Darien, Georgia; published in the 1980s.

**shiftworker:** An operative of The Order, serving 39-day increments in the mission of recovering victims of Temporal Transport.

**Standard Temporal Progression (STP):** Refers to the unaltered progression from past to future, occurring at the regular pace of nature.

**Stinger:** Preferred weapon of CHRON agents.

**Teeson:** Feared leader of an underworld family and CHRON's most wanted criminal for more than twenty-five years.

**Temporal Transport:** A $29^{th}$-century alternative to incarceration. Inmates are gotten rid of by sending them through time, always into the future.

**Tracc:** A portable device used for time travel. There are two types, Auto-Traccs (require compatible power source; can transport up to five people) and Free-Traccs (need no supplemental power; can only transport one person).

**Tracker:** A device implanted in the sole of the foot and used for monitoring location.

**Tram:** A 29th-century form of conveyance.

**Treel:** A device for tracking a person's whereabouts in time but not in space.

**Tysar Effect:** A detrimental disruption of the underlying foundations of time and space. Fear of the Tysar Effect is the reason Temporal Transportees are never sent to the past.

**Unders:** Label given to citizens of the 29th century who refuse to accept the BODs.

**VIC:** A device attached to the wrist, though not below the surface of the skin. They are used for monetary transactions, communication, etc.

**Void Power:** CHRON's misnomer for the Core Power.

**yeeg:** The 29th-century term for "year." The meaning is the same, one Earth orbit around the sun.

**yeeton:** The prevailing power source in the 29ᵗʰ century.

**Zon District:** A suburb of Greeg known for its dangerous network of underworld delinquents.

# Chapter 1

DAY 36

*I hardly know why I write to you. It's not for logic, as everyone has made so clear. I'll never see you again. And soon I won't even know you, won't even know that I don't know you. I'm living in hope, I suppose. You might find this. And if you do—unlikely as that is—maybe you will remember me. Writing to you is the only feeble connection I can find here. Something in me is satisfied to think of you reading this somewhere, in time.*

# Chapter 2

*A modern society hinges on currency. To rebel against currency is to rebel against society.*

**Translated from *The Bulletin*,
CHRON Publication #871476.**

Anac, even as a kid, never sought confrontation. He had two younger brothers. Whenever the inevitable dispute started, he always found somewhere else to go. Almost always. He thought of this as he waited his turn at the Housing Agency, four people in line ahead of him, the green-shine counter drawing nearer and nearer. The first man handed over a slip, the words HOUSING FEE in bold print visible along the top. The clerk was fully bald and wore all white. Like all clerks, he never looked up, not even to receive the paper from the applicant. That was the way of it, Anac thought. When did people quit looking at each other?

This bald clerk studied the card for a moment and then produced from under the counter a small, silver device—a hollow tube, thick walled and open on both ends. Reaching with it across the counter, the clerk touched the applicant on the chest, not at all forcibly. The entire device turned black for about two seconds, then back to silver. With that, he returned the card to the customer and gave a nod of dismissal.

Anac watched all of this in silence. He was surrounded by silence. The un-looking and unspeaking populace. He surveyed the room. Behind him, the gate flashed the ever-scrolling bulletins. The next earthquake was not to hit for another week. Safehouses were closed. The rest of the message focused, as it had yesterday and the day before, on the problem of Unders. The "spreading infection," as *The Bulletin* labeled them. This took Anac's thoughts to Sol, his son. How could anyone call him an infection?

He turned again to face forward in the line. He stared down at his feet, his mind fully on Sol now. The boy will have to grow up in this world. A world each day less and less like the one Anac had known as a child. Maybe giving in, going along, was the best thing for his family now. He was not just taking risks for himself, but for Rachel and Sol as well. But there were risks to giving in, too, he thought.

The next three customers went through the same procedure as the first. Anac put his hands in his pockets to hide the shaking. When it was his turn, he wiped his forehead and removed a card from his pocket, handing it to the clerk.

He kept his eyes down, staring at the floor. While waiting in line he had debated the best course of action. Let them try to get a reading and then tell them? Or tell them up front? Or just hand them his VIC and hope they would accept it? Money is money, he thought—his mind flashing back to the countless times his father had repeated that line. Dad never knew it would come to this, though.

He decided to try. Before the clerk moved his scanner,

Anac reached his left arm across the counter, revealing the VIC banded around his wrist.

The bald man looked up, right into his eyes. "We do not accept those anymore. You know that."

"You bet he knows," a stranger muttered from behind. "He's another Under."

Anac still held his arm extended toward the clerk. He was no longer shaking and was glad of that. Glad and surprised. "I just haven't gotten around to it yet. I know I'm late. How about an exception this time?" He tried a smile. People had told him—Rachel told him—he had a nice smile.

The clerk did not seem to comprehend what he was seeing. "Do you mean to tell us that you have no BOD? Do you know how long that deadline has passed?" The fingers of his free hand were rapping rhythmically against a large green rod resting on the counter.

"Yes, well, I just—"

"Do you or don't you?"

"I don't."

With surprising swiftness the clerk grabbed the rod—a sort of club, thick and heavy—and came down on Anac's arm. The pain caused his knees to give, and as he went down three men in thin helmets, all wearing white, were on him, dragging him toward the exit. They wore the same clothes as the clerk and carried no weapons. They did not need them. Anac was six feet tall and of a sturdy build, but the pain in his arm and the rush of the men had made this no fight at all. With him thrown onto the street, the three turned to go back inside. One looked back just as he reached the door. Anac, rubbing his wrist, looked up at the helmeted stranger.

"Next time we call the CHRONs," the man said, disappearing through the doors.

# Chapter 3

DAY 32

*Knowles said the meeting was at the usual time and place. I rarely went out after dark, but when Knowles wanted to meet I made an exception. You were asleep, and your mother said nothing. She touched my cheek and kissed my forehead and said nothing.*

*Walking alone that night, passing the square buildings in square blocks, the straight rows of trees, I rehearsed my thoughts. I'd told Knowles what happened to me, but he had not told any of the others. I wondered if my experience was the reason for the meeting. Or perhaps others had stories to tell. A lot had been happening lately.*

*What difference does it make if I write of it now? There was always, for me, an escape from my fear. Always. To be honest it feels good to confess it, if only to this piece of paper. What can you liken it to? I don't know. There's nothing like it in this era. Or maybe there is, just in a form I have not yet had time to recognize. I pulled the Lort from my pocket and held it to my eye. Not a care in the world while it lasts. Strangely, not a care in the world while leading up to that moment, except the care to overcome the temptation and hurl the Lort out of sight and out of my life forever.*

*I did not hurl it that night. Like so many nights before I let my right eye breathe it in, and for a time all was well. But something is always lost when that time is over. Something indefinable and important. I lost it that night, and wondered ever after if it caused what came next. My guard down, my mind elsewhere, my strength given over. Possibly—yes, probably—I could have walked a safer path. Yet, here I am.*

# Chapter 4

*There is little danger in what lies ahead. We must only guard what has already passed.*

**Translated from *First Principles*, CHRON Publication #328132.**

The building was fully lit. Buildings were always lit. He found the usual door, unlocked it, and walked in. The hallway was white-walled with a black floor and a black ceiling. Perfectly square, all unfurnished. The bare walls looked just like the hallways of his living quarters.

Sixth door on the right was the stairs. Third floor, left, then to the hall's end. Knowles was waiting.

"Come on—the rest are already inside."

That was unusual.

Knowles was a thin man. Anac thought a breeze might blow him away, but when his feet planted on something, he was immovable. An old man, though he did not look it. Very tall. He overdressed for every occasion, but even more-so for these meetings. Tonight, he wore all red.

He spoke with his usual calm, and then leaned in close to Anac's ear. "Will you share what happened?"

Anac nodded.

"I have a plan. Seven others are agreed, and I hear we are not alone in the community."

"More Unders?"

"Yes. Perhaps many more."

"I doubt it."

Through the door Anac faced the small crowd. All looked at him. No ceremony, just right into it. He told his tale and showed his wounds. " 'Next time we call the CHRONs.' They told me that."

The group nodded in grave response. There were twelve men present, not counting himself. As he finished and went to a chair, the dozen were talking at once. Resuming, it seemed, an argument that had begun before he arrived.

"They'll never let us do that," one man said. Anac had not seen him at any meetings before. He was the only one in the room Anac did not know.

"They won't let us live on here, either," replied Knowles. "It's this or nothing."

"Or just accept the BODs," said the other man.

This sparked a unified disapproval from the rest of the group. Apparently, the majority still agreed on something. People's reasons, he knew, were very different, but the conclusion was the same. BODs were a breach in a profound and deep-seated barrier, a threshold that must not be crossed, with side effects that must not be risked.

"Will someone please fill me in?" Anac asked.

Knowles answered, "The proposal is that we relocate. Start our own community, out of the city and free from the BODs. There is already a secret settlement in the South. We will go peacefully and will sever all ties with CHRON. If we are such a nuisance to them, we will just go."

"A community of twelve?"

"And the families of the twelve. And the others."

"How many others are there?" the stranger spoke up again, this time leaning forward.

"Hard to say," said Knowles. "Some estimate between 100 and 150. Hard to say."

"Where? Where's the settlement?"

"Near Greeg. About a half-day's walk southwest from Greeg."

Anac started to say something here, but the words gelled slowly. He wanted to argue that leaving was a fool's dream. That secession, even peaceful secession, was always seen as sedition.

He never got the words out. Just as he started, the stranger rose and walked to the door, his eyes locked on Anac as he left. His smile was small and unwavering. Anac knew before it happened what was about to happen, but it was too late. The CHRONs washed in, tagged them all, kept them there until nearly morning, then began taking them out of the room one by one. Two agents escorted Anac home to his quarters.

The CHRONs opened his door, un-knocking, and deposited him inside. Rachel rushed to him, letting out a short moan as she wrapped him in a tight hug. He knew what it was—she had seen the blood leaking out of his shoe and knew it meant he had been tagged. A Tracker. She shook. "No. No. No. Anac."

He held two strong arms around her, then stroked her

hair. "We don't know what it means yet. We don't know for sure yet. It's alright."

"What did they say?" she whispered.

"Nothing," he answered honestly. Aside from orders— Move here! Get in there!—the agents had said nothing.

"What does this mean?"

He wanted the look, the fear, to go from her eyes. "I'll have to talk to Knowles. He'll know better. I'm sure it will come to nothing."

Rachel blinked, releasing a single tear. In silence she reached to his arm, just where the blow had been delivered at the Housing Agency, and gently squeezed. He felt the pain on the bruised bone.

"Still," he admitted, "we should have a plan. If—I mean— if something comes up, there is a settlement in the South. Knowles spoke of it. I think maybe you should go there, you and Sol. I don't know."

"Where? I think the three of us should go now."

"No, not now. It's a last resort. I think a CHRON was in the room when we spoke of it last night. Knowles says it's southwest of Greeg. There's a Tram Con to Greeg. Take it on the pretense of portion-trace, and then on foot the rest of the way."

Rachel pulled back Anac's sleeve and looked at his bruise. "Let's go. The three of us. Today."

"We just—"

Shuffling clothing interrupted from the other room. Sol was awake. He stepped into view, dragging his stuffed nighty toy. His brown hair was draped over his right ear, disheveled.

His eyes looked sleepy. "Daddy, where were you? Where were you last night? We waited up late. Daddy?"

Anac rushed to his son and lifted him in a high hug. "Don't worry, bud. Meeting went a little long, that's all. Did you get enough sleep?"

"Yeah."

"Are you wheezing?" he asked, putting his ear up to Sol's chest.

"Just a little."

"I'll get your Proce. Just a second."

Sol squeezed his father's neck and hung there, secure. "I'm glad you're home."

# Chapter 5

*A nation of weaklings, those who fear to praise themselves, is not a nation worth saving.*

**Translated from *Recruit Manual*,**
**CHRON Publication #338272.**

The slick metallic bridge stretched to the vanishing point and was filled with two endless columns of agents marching up the walkway to the Central-Command of CHRON, epicenter of Headquarters. Every off-duty agent was required to attend such ceremonies. A recovery team had returned. Something had gone wrong with two evictees in the year 3184. Intervening forces were operating in later centuries, apparently. CHRON dispatched agents, and then the corpses of both evictees had landed at Headquarters, but that was all. Most thought the recovery team had been lost, perhaps stranded without their Auto-Traccs. But then the three agents landed, safely returned, heroes.

"My glory, all!" countless agents chanted in perfect unison. The three heroes began their long march down this hall of praises. "My glory, all!" the column shouted again. The agents along the sides, like the three in the aisle, were dressed in the black combat suit of the CHRONs.

Of the thousands of throats sending the shout again and

again, only one held silent. Agent Herson of A714 moved his lips to avoid censure—they saw, he knew—but he could not bring himself to speak. He struggled hard against the urge to spit as the three paraded by, those bloated and basking agents of ineptitude, lapping up the glory that should be his. He could have done that mission himself, one man alone. Let them divide the spoils of glory three ways—he would have had it all. All! If only they would give him a chance. A recovery mission. He had applied twenty-nine times, and twenty-nine times been rejected.

"We need to send experience, and you have no experience with recovery," they'd said.

He wanted to ask how he was expected to get experience if they refused to send him.

"You get your missions. Go and do them well."

He obeyed. Did them all well. Not easy missions either. Dangerous assignments—cleaning up the Zon District, dealing with the Teeson family, guarding Tram Con 402. Barely a seventy percent survival rate among agents in such fields. But those jobs were all death and no glory. What he needed was a recovery mission, reserved for the elite of the elite, and glory beyond measure.

"My glory, all!" the chant resounded again in Herson's burning ears.

*When I get one, when it's my turn to walk this parade, I'll be walking alone. Yes, I'll be walking alone.*

"My glory, all!" Herson spoke the last chant aloud, through gritted teeth.

# Chapter 6

*In light of the resultant disorder, we proposed the formation of a council: the Chronological Head-quarters for the Restoration of Normalcy.*

**Translated from *First Principles*,**
**CHRON Publication #328132.**

Anac looked down at the Tram and knew. The three days since the meeting had been an endless strain of watching the windows, listening to the halls, sitting awake long into the night. In three days of debating on whether to flee to Greeg or wait it out, he had repeatedly consoled himself with Knowles's assurance that even if the CHRONs do come—an unlikely move, he predicted—they will only take him. Not Rachel. Not the boy.

The door kicked in and he knew. Thudding boots and faceless soldiers flowed in like a burst dam. They had come for him. Come because of the meeting. Some part of his mind had already settled certain questions, choices that he could not share with Rachel. If they came, he would go peacefully, would walk out without a fight to ensure his family would be spared. That was why he had finally rejected the escape to Greeg. Had they been caught in the flight, which was likely, all three would have been lost. If he was taken quietly in his own living quarters, right where the CHRONs expected and wanted him to be, only he would be lost.

The agents must have sensed his submissiveness, for though they barged in with noise and violence, they apprehended him with something almost like gentleness. They placed him by the door, removed his VIC, and held him in Crane—unable to move his body or even turn his head. He could hear Rachel screaming hysterically somewhere behind. This would probably be her last look at him, and he wanted to seem at peace. Sol's last look at his father, and he wanted to look brave. Then Rachel screeched some words that ripped Anac in half.

"Sol! No! No! No! Sol!" she shouted. There was a pounding and clanging amid the endless shrieking. The boy also was screaming. Anac could not move, could not turn, could not see. But he knew. They were rounding up the boy too.

The agents did much kicking and prodding as father and son were herded down the stairs and onto the platform. Only when they passed the doorway into the crowded Tram car was the Crane released. Anac immediately grabbed for his boy as the door slid shut, their captivity complete.

On the Tram, Anac held tight to Sol's hand as they wedged amid the tightly packed group of prisoners. The boy shook and cried. Rachel had followed them as far as the loading dock. She apparently was not a target. Not today. Anac's eyes met hers through the car's windows. Sol was too short to see, so Anac lifted him, elbowing to make room, to see his mother.

"We love her," he whispered in Sol's ear, "I know Son.

We love her." His tears choked his throat, but nothing could be done. Rachel stared back into his eyes. He mouthed one word, "Greeg," hoping she would go, would at least save herself. The Tram shot out of holding and was up to speed in an instant. He never blinked until the loading dock, his world on it, fell out of sight.

A hand touched his right shoulder. He looked to see Alex, who lived two floors down. Anac did not know that he was an Under. He must have been at secret meetings of his own, or else he would not be here. Presumably, everyone on the Tram had been at meetings somewhere or other. The mistake was obvious—the Unders had doubted their size. At least two hundred were in this car alone.

The group did not sway as the Tram sped off. They did not sway as it turned or jolt as it stopped. Such forces had long since been overcome, as had the appearance of blurred vision when viewing a speeding landscape through a window. Moving or stopped, all was in focus. The CHRONs raced inside another building, armed. Within half an hour, another mob was herded onto the Tram into the next car to the rear. Without any jolt, they were off again.

There were eight such stops, all living quarters. The woman next to Anac fell to her knees and vomited. He tried to comfort her with one hand, his other never releasing his son's grasp.

Anac let go of the kneeling woman as the Tram made its ninth stop. They had arrived at a short building, the first of its kind. The rest had been huge cubes. This one was all curves and points and angles, disorienting to look at in this ninety-degree world. He waited to see the CHRONs rush in, but nothing moved. The people in his car were silent. Those near a window watched. He watched.

Three agents walked toward the building, seeming for the first time less confident in their stride. They went in, and all was still again for several minutes. He knew this place. The steep-sloping roof, the disproportionate peaks, and the unsymmetrical windows made it plain. He knew no one lived here. Buildings of this sort were not dwellings. They were gathering points for The Order. He had never been inside such places.

Anac reached to wipe his nose with a trembling hand. A lone figure came out of the building, Craned, with the three agents behind. There was no sound. He was dressed in all black, but not like the uniform of the CHRONs. His beard was thick and black. He walked to the Tram and boarded a car behind.

# Chapter 7

*There can be no continuance of incarceration.*
*We waste resources and room on those who deserve*
*it least.*

**Translated from *The Bulletin*,**
**CHRON Publication #871293.**

Miles later, another building came into view. Anac had never seen anything so large. Silver, shiny, square, huge. The mammoth doors in the side of the building rolled open as agents began leading the Unders off the Tram car. Single file, eyes down.

The vomiting woman could not rise. Two CHRONs grabbed her.

"I can help her. She'll be fine," Anac pleaded.

"Shut up." And they took her.

The car emptied rapidly. Sol walked in front and held one hand behind, tight in his father's grasp. Anac would not let go of that hand—this he firmly resolved.

He thought of the Lort in his pocket, and hated himself for thinking of it. Alex was two rows to Anac's left and about ten people back. Guards were staggered along both sides of the column, widely spaced. Anac slipped back one position, tugging Sol gently with him, motioning for the boy to be silent. An old man passed. A stranger. Without looking up, he mumbled in a low grunt, "Be careful."

No agent had seen the move. About ten paces later they tried another. The building the prisoners marched toward had not seemed far away, but he saw now this illusion was due to its size. He figured still fifteen minutes or more before they reached the entrance. They marched along a metallic walkway elevated about ten feet above the ground.

He moved again, this time gaining three positions. Alex wore his service clothes, a blue vest over an orange jump suit. His face showed stubble from several days of not shaving. Anac thought back to the day they had taken Alex's wife to the precinct. He felt so sorry for him now, even amid his sorrow for himself.

"Alex," Anac said in a hush, eyes still looking down.

"I'm glad they moved her," Alex replied. "I wasn't sure before, but now I know."

"Yes," Anac said. "Yes, she will miss all this. It will miss her. I am sure of it." A tear dripped from the tip of his nose and onto the platform.

"We were fools," Alex said after two dozen marching paces had gone by. "Did you ever know these numbers?"

"No," Anac said, risking a look at him for a moment, "and I didn't know you were in it—of it, I mean."

"Same."

The entrance to the building was near. The front of the line was already entering a wide cavity. More guards were present than before. Anac was afraid to speak.

"You know where they're taking us?" Alex said, barely audible.

"Not sure," said Anac. He looked down at his hand holding Sol's and said a bit louder, "Probably just going to hold us a while then send us home."

Alex grunted.

"Martha is safe," Anac said.

"Thank you."

Anac was glad he said that. He wanted to say more to comfort his friend and, simultaneously, his son, but he was interrupted by a familiar and terrible noise. His son began to wheeze. Faintly at first, but he knew right away that an attack was forming in the boy's lungs and that the barely audible whistle might well grow to something serious if the medicine were not injected.

Sol held Anac's hand and with his other dug into the pocket of his pants. A look of panic flashed on his face, and with pleading eyes he stared up. He did not have his Proce. Anac had seen enough to know that even a delay in medication led to frightening sounds from the boy's chest, and he'd read enough to know that missing medication could be fatal.

He squeezed Sol's hand, then took a risk.

"Agent!" he shouted. "I need an agent!"

He wondered if they would drag him away as they had the vomiting woman. His great fear since they boarded the Tram was the inevitable moment when he would be separated from his son. His shouting might be speeding them to that horror, but there was nothing else to do.

The nearest agent stomped over and, never stopping the pace of the march, pointed his Stinger into Anac's side.

"Say one more word and you won't say another, ever."

Anac wanted so badly to explain, but he knew from their

reputation that agents were not given to idle threats. He looked to the agent and then to his son—Sol's chest was heaving now—and then back to the agent and then to the boy. He hoped his eyes would communicate enough, hoped that the CHRON would see what was happening. He realized that even if the agent caught on to the crisis, he might not care. Might not act. Might just drag one or both of them away, or perhaps leave them alone to suffer. Leave Sol there, unaided, to choke and maybe die.

The agent, marching alongside the prisoners, said nothing. He reached into a pouch hanging near his waist and pulled out a small canister, silver and smooth, with a tiny conical cap coming to a point at the tip. The agent grabbed Sol by the hair. Anac flinched but restrained his reflex. Then the agent pressed the cone up the boy's nose. If the operation hurt, Sol gave no sign. The agent removed the canister, replaced it in his pack, and walked away without a word. The wheezing stopped.

# Chapter 8

DAY 29

*I remember when I first met Alex and Martha. I was reading on a bench outside my quarters. They were new residents and were being shown the grounds—and taught the rules. They were a good bit younger than me. Happy. I was happy then, too.*

*Rachel and Martha really hit it off. They cooked together. That was their thing. Peculiar really, since Rachel was so particular about cooking. She had a way of—but I don't want to talk about that. I can't.*

*Alex and I reaped the reward. He would get home from the Exchange, still in uniform, and knock on my door. He'd tell me the gals were at it again. You, cuddled in my lap, would look up at me and grin. Both of us knew a feast awaited downstairs.*

*All food is eaten cold in our home time. A hot meal just prepared must then be flashed until chilled to right before the point of freezing. We never cared for eating food any other way. No one did. Funny how things come to be normal that were never normal before.*

*You always sat to my right. Such a big eater! You would finish your portion and I would slip you some of mine, some bit I didn't care for. Would pass it to your plate with a wink, a smile.*

*Enough of that. All is in the past now. My past. Soon to be forgotten.*

*Sol, are you still a big eater? Do you still prefer your food cold, even in this age of warm meals? Son, can you remember?*

# Chapter 9

*Results confirm that forty days after Transport, the memory is wiped, rendering Traccs useless. Agents with a Gor-Implant will not suffer this side effect. It is imperative that the populace not know any of this. There is enough opposition to Temporal Transport as it is.*

**Translated from *The Bulletin*,
CHRON Publication #871307.**

Whatever the agent had done wholly healed the wheeze. Apparently they wanted everyone alive. For now. Anac shook at the prospect of continuing this horrible journey without a Proce. His own chest nearly locked up at the thought of the boy being alone—separated from Mom and Dad—caught in another wheezing fit, unable to call for help, unable to help himself.

The shadow of the gaping door covered them as they entered the building. The CHRONs began separating them into groups of roughly twenty. Anac held tightly to Sol's shoulders. The prisoners never stopped walking. The large hall forked, and a group of Unders was silently led down the side corridor. Then another fork, and another. They separated

Alex's group at the eleventh split. Fifty paces later, Anac and Sol and several others were led down a passage to the right.

The agents marched them for what seemed an impossibly long time until finally they told the group to stop and face the wall. Agents spaced them out at arm's length. Sol stood to the left of his father. Anac could see the boy trembling. Both faced the bare white wall. Anac's left hand squeezed tightly to Sol's right. He heard the footsteps thud behind them and stop.

"Let it go," the voice said.

Anac squeezed and said nothing. They would have to chop off his hand before he let go of his son.

The agent did not say more. Anac felt the thunderbolt in his spine, his muscles locking, wrenching, gripping with a force he thought might shatter all his bones. The jolt lasted only seconds, but it held in it the pain of a lifetime. When it ended, he went limp and fell to the floor. He knew he had been shot with a Stinger, not set to kill but to stun. Strong arms lifted him back to his feet. He looked at Sol and saw an agent behind the boy. Anac dared not reach out again for fear they might stun his son. He stood still and silent until the agents walked down the line. Sol was crying with short, gasping heaves of his tiny chest.

Minutes passed. Anac marveled at how such a debilitating pain could be completely relieved in so short a time. Aside from the memory, he felt now as if he had never been stunned. The memory, though, was enough. More silent minutes passed in cornered desperation. He wanted his boy's hand back. He wanted out. He wanted Rachel. He cut his eyes, head still down. The Unders with him, strangers all, began to seem a faint hope. Strength in numbers, he thought. Ludicrous, but something. He felt he should call out to them, but he could not forget the Stinger.

He heard thumping sounds from both ends of the line of prisoners. He knew the sound. Doors were opening.

He needed to know what was happening, what was coming. Sol looked into his eyes, appealing tears on his cheeks. Dads were supposed to protect, supposed to be able to do something. He felt like a man in an earthquake, wanting badly to grab his family, to clutch his loved ones, to get them to safety, but instead only standing with frozen arms and paralyzed legs, unable to move or reach out as the earth swallowed them all away forever.

Unders disappeared as agents pushed them one by one into the opening doors. Thump-thump-thump, a door would open. Then thump-thump-thump it would close, and one more person would be missing. He counted three CHRONs guarding this shrinking group. Two on each end and one in the middle near where he stood. If the pattern continued, he would be the last led through a door. He would have to watch his son pushed away.

Each agent held a Stinger. Ten Unders remaining. Anac shut his eyes tight. *Think,* he told himself. *Think.* Six remaining. Thump-thump-thump. Boots pounded, nearer, nearer. *Think!*

Three remaining. Sol to the left, a stranger to the right, himself in the middle. What was courage? And did he have any? Thump-thump-thump.

A shot of boldness. "What is this all about?" he managed,

his voice fighting a tremble, attempting confidence. Sol stood before an open door, a hungry black mouth. The boy's eyes locked on Daddy, his chest heaving. The agents' heads turned toward Anac. He hated them. Their coldness. Their ridiculous armor, always blank and black. Taking him from his wife. Taking his boy from Mom and Dad. He spoke again.

"You drag us out of our homes and force us here. And for what? Because we won't accept a BOD? What difference does it make? Keep me with my son!"

Normally, he felt sure, a prisoner would not have finished the sentence. A Stinger would have ended either his consciousness or his life depending on the setting. But the moment was interrupted. A thump-thump resounded from up the hallway. All six heads—three prisoners and three guards—turned to look. The sound continued and grew louder. It was not the thump-thump of a door. These were footsteps, fast ones. Around the corner came a man with a torn and bloodied shirt. He was barefoot and ran with a limp.

Three Stingers went up as the three prisoners watched. Anac reached and covered Sol's eyes. The bloodied man stopped in a sudden fall. Two agents rounded the corner behind him, heavy boots thudding then halting. The man was caught in the middle. He was in full panic.

"Do you know what they're doing to us?" he yelled from the floor. "It's—" But the Stingers went to work from both sides. The man shook briefly and was still. Silent. Smoldering.

Anac took the opportunity of this distraction to grab his son in a hopeless and profound hug. Thump-thump-thump. Doors opened. The agents pried them apart. "Dad—Dad—

Dad—Dad!" Sol screamed as their arms were torn from this last embrace.

"Dad!"

They tossed Anac into his dark cell, alone, and the door thump-thump-thumped, sealing shut.

# Chapter 10

DAY 27

*I'm more alone than ever now, Sol. The shiftworker had to leave. It was his last day. The only companion I have left is my writing. Somehow it makes me feel closer to you. He left me a book.* First Principles. *I've had some time to read it. It answers so many questions.*

# Chapter 11

*Envisioning the Void Power as an entity all its own is but a metaphor for functions we don't yet understand. There is, of course, nothing there, and we will understand all soon enough.*

**Translated from *First Principles*,
CHRON Publication #328132.**

Anac did not know how long he'd been in the dark, solitary cell. His sense of time was muddled by two things. One, the despair of being separated from Sol. It crazed him. He felt as if he were spinning in rapid circles as the room, rooted firmly in the ground, blurred around him. Then he felt as if he were pressed down to the floor by heavy weights. Sturdy reality loosed from its bindings and spun away—away and up into fog and darkness. His vision blurred with tears upon tears as he pounded his head against the hard metal of his cell, nearly enough to concuss himself. "This isn't happening, this isn't happening, this isn't happening," he said over and over and over as time crawled by.

The second reason he lost his temporal bearings was, to his shame, the temptation of the Lort. In the deep darkness, the lure to grab at any faint light was strong, and he found his mind ever going to his pocket. He knew what was in there.

"No," he told himself. "Sol. Sol. Sol. Sol." But his son—his only son, his beloved son locked in some dark cell awaiting some dark fate—sometimes would slip from the forefront of his mind and be replaced by thoughts of the Lort. "Sol, Sol, Sol," he kept saying, forcing his mind to stay where a father's mind ought to stay. But then, once again, the Lort.

These thoughts eventually gave way to action—he reached into his pocket, retrieved the Lort, and brought it to his eye. As he released the trigger, all worries faded. Sol and CHRON vanished completely. The darkness of the cell became the comfort of a quilt. The wrongs were righted in a blink. The spinning of the room was the rocking arms of sleep. He had the vividness of waking and the peace of sleeping and in that moment he was happy.

But that moment did not last. Time, refusing to slow its incessant march forward, brought him back to reality soon enough, and afterwards the cell seemed tighter, its darkness more complete, his plight more hopeless than ever before. He could not bring himself to move off the floor, to care about his next breath, so great was his shame.

Thump-thump-thump. A door opened. He wondered if it was the same door he had entered through. He had a sense that it was on the opposite side of the cell, but he was disoriented and unsure. A pale yet intense light flooded his chamber, which he now saw to be an empty square, and two agents entered. They lifted him to his feet.

As they led him into the light, their hands under his arms, he saw it was not the hallway from before, the place where he had last seen Sol. This room was spherical, and full of women. A high platform with a golden desk rose along the left side, and all the rest of the sphere's interior was peopled with gray-clad females, venerable and powerful. Something in the look of their faces spoke of authority. They all stood. Every eye stared at him as he was led in front of the golden desk, over which glared the eyes of President Leeson himself. Anac recognized him at once from the hundreds of images displayed over the city—that unmistakable bandage on his head, a deep wound, so the rumors said. He had never seen Leeson in person, had never expected to, and he wanted more than anything not to be seeing him now.

Leeson spoke, eyes locked on Anac. "You know why you are here, and you will find out soon enough why we are here." Leeson swept his hand over the silent crowd and droned on. "The BODs are a beacon of our society. Our hope is in the wisdom of our commerce. Do you have any idea what we have built here? What it would be without us? You Unders want to reject all that we have built. You are charged with the grave offense of this rejection. Have you anything to say?"

*Where's my son? Where's my son? Let me see my son!* was all Anac thought to say. When he spoke, though, all he actually said was, "Sol?"

"You want to see him? The moment to give your defense and you waste words on that? Do you know where you are? My glory."

Anac bowed his head, saying nothing.

"You reject BODs, yes?"

"Not reject! No. You all go ahead. We just want to do things a different way—an older way."

"To dislike is to rebel. Tell me 016, what made you reject the simplest of decrees? What is it about the BODs?"

Anac had asked himself this question countless times. With all the risks involved in refusing BODs, and leading his wife and son to refuse them, he had surveyed his motives carefully. And with each survey he badly wanted to find a loophole, a justification, a way to simply go along with the decree and the CHRONs and the mass of society.

"President Leeson, have you read Hikerson?"

"I executed Hikerson."

Anac fumbled for words. The agents flanking him on both sides stepped closer, showing that the time for silence had expired.

"Well, Hik—I mean, research has shown that bloodstream-based implants affect the mind irreversibly. Studies of the BOD's only predecessor—the GIDs of 2763—concluded that within the first year, subjects of the implant were wholly new personalities. What they liked before they liked no more. Whom they loved before they could no longer abide. Everything changed. The process was unavoidable and irreversible." Anac was surprised at his own candor. Somehow he felt if ever faced with such questioning—he had long feared this day—he would lie. Would try to cover himself as he did at the Housing Agency. "I forgot," or "My cells rejected the first attempt," or any such excuse seemed better than spilling his true fears, which as he aired them now felt more like direct accusations against CHRON.

He never meant to accuse, but simply to avoid. Truly, the thought of losing his personality, his very self, had scared him from the start, and even now scared him more than what-ever they were about to do to him. "But none of this is Sol's fault. He's so young. He just does what his daddy does. He is as good a citizen as CHRON ever knew."

"016, your misinformation will cost you dearly. The GIDs were another matter entirely, and the propaganda you've read on them has never been substantiated. The BODs are merely a way to exchange currency. But I am not here, we are not here," and again he swept his hand over the room, "to debate with you Unders. We are here to pass sentence. Temporal Transport. To be carried out immediately."

At that moment, President Leeson vanished. He said his last word and blipped out of existence. Anac realized he had not been speaking with Leeson at all, but merely with a Module. This made sense, he saw now, considering the number of Unders arrested today. Leeson would not take the time to meet them all.

On the opposite side of the room from where Anac had entered, a wide door thump-thump-thumped open. Six chairs were lined along the center of the newly opened passage. Only the sixth was empty. The fifth held Sol. Anac struck out in a mindless dash toward him.

He made only two steps before that same horrible shock, a Stinger stun as in the hallway, pelted him. This time even harder than before. When he came to, he was in the sixth chair, Craned so that only his eyes could move. He cut them hard to the right and could see Sol's feet, but that was all.

A countdown was underway, nearly complete. The mech-anized voice rolled on, "Eight...seven...six." *This can't be*, he thought. *It's not fair. It's not fair. It's not fair.* He knew enough of Temporal Transport to know that no two prisoners were ever sent to the same time. That was the whole point of the process, to remove the unwanted. To remove them from their present society, and to remove them from each other. Rumors of the horrid side effects of being sent through time, being deposited into some future moment and marooned there forever, were widespread. No one could verify, because no one but CHRON agents ever jumped time and actually returned, and CHRON was perfectly secretive about such information.

*It's not fair. It's not fair. It's not fair!* To be so irrevocably separated and not even allowed a last look at his boy. "Three...two." Never to see him again, and now only allowed a look at his feet. *It's not fair! It's not fair!* His mind screamed. Being Craned, his mouth could not utter a sound any more than his head could make a move.

"One."

The air turned thick, like water, then gel, then water again. It was hard to see even Sol's feet in the blur. Sound was not blurred, though. It was amplified and made more vivid. Anac could hear the countdown, but there must have been some distortion, for the numbers were out of sequence.

"Sixteen...seven...fourteen...nine...seven...seven." The air that was water felt too thick to breathe, but he realized also that he was not breathing. Sol was farther away than before, his feet a dim haze in a submersed blur. Then something broke. Some dam loosed and the air that was water rushed upward, sucked straight toward the ceiling. But there was no ceiling, only darkness. He could hear clearly, but it was no longer the monotone countdown. There was shouting. He thought that this must be it. The water was being sucked away into the darkness and he would be sucked with it, jolted through time to whatever futuristic nowhere he had been sentenced.

But this did not happen. The water went away, yet he remained Craned in the chair. He rolled his eyes in every direction, maddened by his limited range of vision. Beyond Sol's feet, agents were firing. He wondered what they could possibly be firing at. And then he was loose. Just like that. The Crane was released and he was loose.

Instinctively, he made a lunge for his son. As he did, he saw what the agents were doing. Some were watching the door, Stingers ready. Others were firing into the chairs, executing the Unders. Something had gone wrong. He jumped on top of Sol in a faint hope to block the shots from him. The boy could neither move nor talk. Anac covered him. "I got you, Son." He put his hand over Sol's eyes.

Then the agents turned to the door as it thumped open. Rushing through it was someone Anac immediately recognized. It was the bearded man who had boarded the Tram alone, the one from The Order. He blitzed into the room and somehow went untouched by the Stingers. The agents were firing and firing, but he was not brought down. Anac held his hand tight over Sol's eyes as the man with the beard tossed something in among the agents. Then a flash of light, bright and unbearable, then the waters returned and the air disappeared and the darkness came and Sol was gone.

# Chapter 12

*The Tysar Effect might be negated if the distur-*
*bance is removed before the memory is wiped. There*
*is something fundamental about the forty days that*
*we do not yet understand.*

**Translated from *The Bulletin*,**
**CHRON Publication #871307.**

Agent Herson looked at the buildings speeding by the
Tram. He was in a CHRON-Car. Agents only. The speed
was intense but nothing blurred. Scenery flying by outside
the windows was as in focus as if he had been stationary.
Herson mused on the distant past, the days of black smoke
and wooden wagons, iron beasts and exploding rifles. For
the hundredth time in his life he grunted in disgust at the
ignorance of the other agents. None studied history beyond
the gibberish taught at the Academy. They knew nothing,
yet they still got the coveted recovery missions while he had
to sit around counting his twenty-nine rejected applications
and filing his twenty-nine appeals.

This trip, though, might be something. Never had President Leeson himself contacted Herson about an appeal, and
the urgency of the message felt real enough.

One identical cubic building after another shot by, each

a clone of the other. There were no people on the loading ramps or walkways. Work-Time was in, and all outdoor spaces would stay deserted until the Pulse went out from Headquarters. *Then*, thought Herson, *the mindless herd will stagger home, going from nothing to nowhere and back again. Glory-less.*

The Tram stopped, and Herson walked out of the empty car and up the empty bridge that led into Headquarters. Two unmoving agents flanked the side of Leeson's door. Herson knew better than to waste time talking to either of them, so he sat on a bench across the hall and spent the silence guessing what this might be about.

The door to Leeson's office shot open. An agent, not in uniform, walked out hurriedly, eyes down at his feet.

"Your turn," was the monotone command of the tallest of the two guards.

Herson rose and walked into the coolness of the office, noting, as he entered, the intensity of the light inside. He had never been in this room, but he had heard rumors of the president's Lort addiction and the subsequent weakening of his eyesight after many years of the indulgence. The president stood in the center of the mostly bare room, his bandage clearly visible, and waited for the salute. Herson kneeled. "My glory, all," he said.

"Louder," Leeson demanded, as was his custom.

"My glory, all!" Herson said with conviction.

"Remain."

For the rest of the conversation, Herson never rose from his knees and never looked up. Leeson walked to the far side of the room, so far that he had to speak loudly to be heard, and from a black and green seat he spoke to Herson in slow, deliberate sentences, as one might speak to an ignorant child. All of this Herson had somewhat expected, basing his predictions on the endless rumors that circulated about Leeson's ways. Still, the air of condescension was thick and hard to breathe.

"You've heard of the blast yesterday," Leeson said, his tone indicating he did not want a reply. "There were six in the room. We were able to kill four. A real tragedy, that. Two more dead and we would not have anything to worry about. It appears the attack was not well coordinated—none of the other Temporal Transport Rooms were infiltrated."

Leeson paused and Herson took the opportunity to say something that he knew the president would like. "That's just like The Order," Herson said. "No real plan, no real organization."

"As if you know anything about it. Anyway, two were mid-Transport, and the blast did not cripple the machine as I suppose the fool wanted. You know The Order's stance on Temporal Transport. These two, a father and son, were in the same chair when it happened. So they have landed either in the same time, or within ten years of one another."

"That's unconventional, sure. But is it really a problem?"

Leeson paused several moments before speaking. "The peculiarity is, our Treels tell us the two Unders were sent to the past."

Herson forgot himself and looked up. A hard glare from Leeson put his eyes back on his feet. "My glory, all," he said, apologizing. But his mind was running. *The past,* he thought. *What could this mean? The implications of this. What about the Tysar Effect? When was the last time something—?*

Leeson interrupted, "Recovery teams had a fairly low survival rate in the early years. The process has been perfected now, and in truth is hardly needed at all. When it is, our agents always come back. Almost always. But this, well, this is different. This mission is as good as suicide."

*So you finally have one for me, is that it?* Herson thought.

"We have one for you. Twenty-nine applications and rejections, this should be pleasant news for you, right Herson?"

"Of course, sir. And I will— "

"Shut up. We're sending you because we don't want to waste our best. You and two rookies not even out of the Academy. The highest compliment I can give any of you three is that you're expendable."

"When do we leave?"

"The two others of your team, Parkson and Tagson, are already in Transport Room 502. You will go there now. They'll tell you your destination year. Don't worry, it's an electrical age. Electrical enough, anyway. As usual, two corpses will be just fine."

This was happening fast. "May I wrap up a few details in my office before I go?"

"Oh, whatever," Leeson grunted, "just be quick. Negson wants to know what I'm doing about this issue, and he won't leave me alone until I give him something progressive. Frankly, we're not sure what will happen if these two Unders are still in the past when their memory is wiped. There's the

Tysar, you know. You get them both back here before the forty-days, is that clear?"

"I won't disappoint you," Herson said.

"Fine. Fine. It's a big step for you, really. If you survive this, you can't imagine the glory for the three of you upon your return."

"Yes," Herson said, "yes, glory for the three of us."

# Chapter 13

Anac was alone in a bright, grassy wood. He pressed his chest tight to the ground, staying well hidden in the green weeds. The height of the trees made him dizzy. He had never seen trunks so thick, nor a forest so scattered. Nothing in rows. Trees strewn about chaotically. And the noise. He thought of holding his ears to drown out the sounds— ceaseless chirping and scampering and shaking. He could not see the sun through the leafy canopy above, but the tangled branches waving in the wind permitted light beams in a blinking strobe unlike anything he had ever seen. Above the treetops, the sky seemed empty, somehow, as if there were no Helts at all.

*Sol*, he thought, but dared not speak aloud. Who might be around in a wood like this he could only guess. He rose onto his elbows, lifting his head just above the grass, and looked around for a sign of his son.

"This can't be the future," he whispered aloud. But the CHRONs do not send to the past. The noises and movements in these woods could not overcome a ripping sense of isolation. He felt deeply alone. He wondered if CHRON had banished him to a time of no people. Maybe that was what Temporal Transport was really about. Or maybe the blast—

His mind reeled from these thoughts, and his frame was

still reeling from the experience of the Transport itself when the sneezing started. Just one at first. It felt strange. He had sneezed maybe four times in his life. Then a second—unprecedented, two sneezes on the same day. Then his head and chest and nose and mouth let loose a torrent of nasal eruptions that he feared might be fatal. Anac curled over in the confusion of such an onslaught. His nose burned, itched, oozed. When the fit finally slackened, he looked up.

Gathering nerve, he called out for the boy. "Sol!" He listened. "Sol!" He paused again. "SOL!" His call was answered by the rolling of drums coming from within the forest. They were unlike any he had ever heard, and seemed far off. They grew in volume rapidly. They were drawing nearer. Something in their rattle, in the way they stung his ears, was otherworldly. Then the horrid drums were interrupted by the sharp blast of a horn. Then more drums, faster than before.

And closer. Ever closer.

Fear tied him to the grass and he pinched his nose hard as it burned. He dared not sneeze again. Dared not make a sound. The drums were roaring now. *I don't want to be here, I don't want to be here, I don't want to be here.*

Then the earthquake hit. Must have been an earthquake, though it felt different than the weekly events he was used to. His whole body, sprawled on the ground, felt the force of it, and a thick tree dropped sharp cones on his back. He bit his lip. Then another shock, as violent as the first, and painfully loud.

The drums must have stopped, or he could simply not

hear them over the horrid ringing in his ears. He felt two or three more quakes, shaking his stomach.

Then he saw what he would gladly not have seen. Natives of this time, whoever or whatever they were. The air around them smoked, and over the ping in his ears he thought he could hear another high yell, as if from a thousand voices. Still trying to keep below the grass, he saw them, more and more of them. Gray figures coming in a full sprint toward him. Time began to creep. He felt he could count to a hundred between each of his panting breaths. He could watch a cone fall from limb to land and years might pass between. He felt light.

He saw each stride of each person—for they were human —as the line ran toward him. He could see every stitch on the gray jackets. The gray caps with black brims. The long weapons, Stingers or spears or something.

Before he thought to run, he was running.

# Chapter 14

DAY 24

*I later learned what 1860s American soldiers look like. What a cannon is. An Enfield. Gunpowder. You cannot imagine what the noise did to me. The boom and bang. Nothing is that loud in the 2800s. Stingers make  hardly any noise at all.*

*I had been afraid on the Tram, but no fear before or since matches how I felt sprinting through that strange wood, thinking you might be out there also, alone.*

# Chapter 15

The line of men spewed fire. Pop, pop, pop. The forest was aflame with smoke and noise. Anac weaved around trees as he careened forward. All was speed and fear. He wondered why he was not hit. A Stinger would have taken him down by now.

A ditch came into view ahead, steep dirt walls on both sides. The gap looked manageable. Beyond it, the trees ended and a sunlit meadow sloped away. He thought if he could make it to the low end of the hill he might be able to change directions, out of their view, and lose his pursuers.

He neared the ditch and readied himself for the jump. His breath was strained, and in his chest something felt torn.

He leapt, hitting his ribs on the top of the far bank of the ditch. He grabbed dirt and roots in a clawing effort to get his lower half out of the trench. The impact had knocked the breath out of him. The pain somehow converted his terror to a strange and strong feeling of guilt, like a child when caught amid a serious infraction.

He rolled and staggered to his feet just as another volley unleashed behind him. He threw himself on the ground to dodge whatever projectiles were coming. Then he was up running again. The end of the tree line was near.

The woods had grown oddly quiet after the last blast. He

sprinted on, bit by bit regaining his breath. At the edge of the meadow he dared to stop and look back into the silent trees. There on the far side of the creek stood a line of men in gray, looking like ghosts, leaning on their weapons and staring. Several pointed at him.

He turned and stepped into the field, not knowing what to do. To his left was an army of men in blue coats standing bolt upright. One of them was shouting. Several carried large flapping sheets on thin poles. His mind screamed to run, but his legs did not obey. His feet seemed rooted.

Large machines, black and metallic, stood among the blue men. Someone shouted, and the machines exploded simultaneously. The smoking beasts shook the ground like a building dropped from the sky. Anac rolled backward from the blast and landed on his back, his head hitting against a stone. All went dark.

From out of the woods on the far side of the meadow, a lone figure appeared. He was wearing the same gray as the men across the creek. His horse galloped. The man wore a sword on one side and a revolver on the other.

He drew his mount to a quick stop next to the unconscious body of the stranger. Looking up, he could see down the twenty-plus barrels staring at him as the men in blue frantically reloaded. He waved toward them but received no answer. Each kept working his cannon. The gray men at the creek were beginning to wade across, but they moved slowly.

Dismounting, he lifted the unconscious stranger from the ground and threw him somewhat roughly over his saddle, facedown. He remounted and gave the horse a kick. He made full speed toward the woods across the meadow, leaving behind the men at the creek and the cannons on the ridge. The shadows of the pines were just covering him when the cannons let go another roar, but he and his charge were now in the trees, and there he slowed and began to work his way back to camp. The easier pace allowed him to relax his grip on the stranger, and using his free hand he pulled a cell phone from his pouch and called the hospital.

# Chapter 16

Anac woke from the awful dream that was no dream. He remembered passing out in the field, under the bright sun of midday. Now as he blinked and tried to grab hold of the situation, it was night. He was inside—locked inside, he presumed—some sort of small vehicle with windows all around. No, not exactly. He soon realized there were glass windows on two sides, but only empty holes on the other two sides. He did not move, fearing to give away that he was awake, hoping somehow to make an escape. Instinctively, he searched his pocket for a Lort. Nothing. He surveyed the side holes, estimating that he could fit through and then make a run for it.

The sky was black, but there was a golden glow around him. Its source, he now saw, was from a glowing instrument mounted atop a large, cylindrical pole. Then he heard the voices. Someone was talking. Low voices, above a whisper but not at conversation level. Two people, a man and a woman. He listened.

"—I don't get you," the female voice said. "Check him in, call the police, see what they know. What if there's already a report out for him, missing person or something?"

"No, I can't do that," the male replied.

"Well, I don't get you, but of course whatever you think is best."

"Thanks, Melanie. Really, thank you."

"So, what are you going to do?" she asked.

"Well, if you really think he is alright—"

"No kidding, healthiest person I've ever seen, if he'll just come to. Really. If he wakes up, I imagine he'll be, well, fine. Finer than fine. It's strange, but he seems—"

She softened her voice, and Anac could not make out the rest of her sentence. The man's voice resumed.

"Well, if he's good, in that sense, I think I'll take him home with me."

"I don't get it. Let's just take him inside. We're not busy tonight. We'll get him put up in a room. Besides, what are you going to tell Miranda?"

There was silence for a time after this question. Anac assumed he was the topic under discussion, though he was not sure what it all meant. The quiet made him uneasy. His mind raced. He couldn't afford to stay captured and detained. Sol had most likely been sent through time, and perhaps by some millionth chance had been sent to this same time—perhaps more likely, he told himself, since it was the same chair. That meant Sol might be out there in those woods. Anac knew enough about Temporal Transport to know that sending-locations determined receiving-locations. He didn't understand it, but remembered reading the histories, how that had been the last major obstacle before mankind finally pierced the time barrier, the obstacle of coordinating time and space minutely enough to accommodate a survivable landing.

He raised his head high enough to see out the window into the artificially lit night. He saw a man in gray uniform and high black boots talking to a woman in some sort of greenish robe or cloak. Behind them was a low white building, haphazard in shape, the words EMERGENCY ROO glowing brightly along an otherwise dark wall. He felt a strange comfort in recognizing a bit of the language. "Roo" he could not explain, but clearly "emergency" was akin to a word from his own time, with just a slight variation in spelling. But this small comfort did not alter his resolve, and tightening his jaw he leapt for the open hole in the side of the vehicle.

His thought was to dive out, catch himself on his hands, and take off running for any dark cover he could find. However, as soon as his head cleared the gap—his momentum too much to allow him to stop—he realized he was higher off the ground than he'd guessed. What he had pictured in his mind as a graceful dive, maybe a roll and then a run, turned into an awkward fall that sent a pop and pain through his left wrist and up his arm. He cried out involuntarily, and though he did not look to see what the others were doing, he knew they had heard, and he figured they were after him.

His feet snagged on the lower edge of his exit hole. He twisted them free, and with a half fall, half roll was finally on the ground. Then off again, up and running without a word or a look back. The explosions and shouts and cries from the nightmare woods of his initial landing reverberated in his memory. Any moment now he expected to hear them all, to hear worse things yet, rising up behind him. He ran on, a straight path into the night, leaping over a small ditch that was well lit from another artificial light above. The ground across the ditch was more of that hard, black material that had popped his wrist when he dove from the vehicle, and figuring this to be a better footing than the dark grasses beyond, he stayed on the road and ran as fast as he could.

He did not hear any pounding of feet or firing of weapons behind him. Still, he felt chased. Certainly he was being chased. After a sustained sprint into and out of patches of light and dark, he made a quick dash to the right. The road was mostly lined with small buildings, but here was a thin sliver of shadowy woods. He could not sprint forever, and he hoped that if he could find a bit of concealment he might venture a look back to see the status of his pursuers.

Limbs slapped hard against his face as he ran into the darkened thicket. The trees here were far smaller and more densely packed than those in the woods of his first landing. Then, with a hard and painful jolt, his right shin struck with the speed of a full run into something solid and sharp. He fell to the leafy ground and pressed both hands on the injury, feeling lightheaded with pain. He looked back toward the street, still in view through the vegetation, and saw he was not actually being pursued. He resolved to lie there, still and silent, until the pain passed. He examined what he had hit. It was a four-wheeled metal contraption, somewhat red.

No sound for the moment. He remained still—watching, listening. He pinched his nose hard trying to silence a gathering fit of sneezes before they erupted. A brightly lit object zoomed past on the black road. A vehicle similar to the one he had just escaped. He deduced immediately that these must be the means of conveyance for people in this era. No Trams or drigs. The smoking weapons in the earlier woods, the wilderness in which he now hid, the nature of the vehicles—all pointed to the same conclusion. This must be the past. He shuddered at the thought. CHRON never sent to the past. Not for prisoners, not for agents, never. Yet, here he was. It must have been something in that blast, some disruption, and if so, what could that mean for Sol? Where would his boy be after a thing like that?

The hopelessness darkened like the night, was darkening further still, when he heard the voice.

"I'm not coming in," a man said from somewhere along the wood's edge. "I'm not coming in, and you can stay in there as long as you need. I'm trying to help."

"Who are you?" Anac asked.

"Whoa, what an accent," the man replied. "Can't wait to hear where you're from. I'm Samuel. I picked you up out the field where you got knocked out."

"Knocked out?"

"Yeah, earlier today. The reenactment field. I guess those cannons gave you a bit of a shock. They're loud enough to stop a heart, I know. Then the rock you hit. But Melanie checked you out. You're alright. It's alright."

"Who is Melanie? Who *are* you?"

"Melanie's a nurse at the Corston Hospital, there across the street. She was on duty tonight so I brought you by. You had me scared being unconscious. I wanted to make sure everything was okay with you, then we could figure what to do next."

Anac said nothing. The man's voice, whoever he was, had a reassuring tone. More of Alex's sort than an agent's.

"Listen, I know this must be strange for you, but maybe I can help get that sorted out, if you want. Of course, I'll leave you alone if you want that too. If you never want to hear from me again, you got it. But, if there's anything you need—"

"Was there a boy with me?" His pulse sped at the question.

"A boy?"

"Yes, six years old, dressed just like me. Brown hair. Was he there?"

"No, you were alone."

"Did you look around, nearby, the woods, anywhere?" His voice was growing in volume, rising in pitch.

"I didn't, bud. I'm sorry. Was he supposed to be with you?"

"Yes! At least, I'd hoped so. My son."

"Oh. Wow. Hey, come on out, come with me. I can call some of the guys and see if they saw anything, anyone, I mean. We were all over those woods, my regiment. If your boy was there, they would have seen him."

This dim hope shined brighter than no hope. He rose and walked, limping slightly, toward the voice of the man called Samuel.

# Chapter 17

DAY 19

*There is a detachment to despair that I did not expect. Reality is often like that, I suppose. "Of course the heavier object falls faster." Until it doesn't. I teamed up with a complete stranger that night and had as little fear about it as if I were paying a visit to Alex.*

*Time is the greatest distance, and in that sense I was as isolated as a man could be. Samuel offered community to replace my isolation. Moreover, he held the only possible (however improbable) hope of finding you. That fact bridged the widest gaps.*

*Not that I was a fool about it. Already I knew my language was somewhat different from his, and I expected my accent was nothing anyone in this age had ever heard. Also, I figured with reasonable certainty that I was in a century that predated the fracturing of the timeline. This meant that telling my story, my real story, would— well, I didn't know exactly what it might mean. At best, these people might think I was insane. At worst, hard to say.*

*Apart from the truth, I could think of little else to tell. Even if I were not an honest man, I knew that trying to fabricate a believable story in an age I knew nothing about was futile. They would see right through it. Then an idea came. It would not be much of a fake for me to play the amnesiac. If they asked how I ended up in those woods, I simply would not remember. Of course, it would be a brand of amnesia that allowed me to remember you. I needed Samuel for that, for the search. Let them think that was all I remembered—in truth, it was all I thought about. That and one other thing: I needed to know the date.*

# Chapter 18

Samuel spoke for several minutes into a sort of handheld VIC, what he called a cell phone. Then he made another call, talked a while, then another, and another. Each time saying much the same thing. "The guy today at the reenactment…Yeah he's with me. Long story…Fine. Did you see a boy out there? He said he had his son with him." These calls repeated themselves as Anac sat on the cushioned bench inside the strange vehicle that Samuel called a truck. The lights on the side of the hospital still lit up the darkness, and with this chance for a closer inspection, Anac realized that the word was actually ROOM, only the M had gone dark. The language gap was not as wide as he had supposed.

Finally, Samuel put his cell phone in his pocket and looked at him. "I'm sorry, Anac, no one saw a boy. You were the only one, and these guys were all over those woods."

He stared out the window into the night without replying.

"The men said you were lying on the ground when they saw you. Jerry said he couldn't figure how you came to be there. He had just been over that spot and not seen anyone."

"Yeah, strange to say I don't know. But I don't know."

Samuel looked at him, then out the front glass toward the empty parking lot. "Maybe you've got memory loss of some kind?"

"Yeah, maybe." Anac was pleased that the lie started naturally.

"Listen," Samuel went on, "you need a place to sleep. Sleep always does a man good. I can take you to my house for tonight, and we can go search those woods ourselves in the morning." He paused, tapping his fingers on the top of the wheel in front of him. "But my wife is not used to people staying over. I mean, neither of us are. It's just not something we... The point is, when we get to my house, do you mind waiting outside while I talk to her? You know, to explain who you are and all that?"

"I don't mind."

"Thanks," and Samuel pulled a lever next to the round wheel. With that, the truck began to move. "If you get cold, I'll let the window up. This uniform's just so hot."

The vehicle was nothing like Trams or drigs, all he had ever known. This device required no track, and it was small. A squishy bench in the front was all it contained, and behind that a sheet of glass that overlooked an empty tub obviously meant to carry cargo. Two beams of light shined over the road ahead. Anac sat on the far right side next to an open hole. The blur of the trees and houses outside was a sight he had never seen. Also, the sway of his body as Samuel drove around turns, or slowed to a stop—all of these forces were hidden when riding a Tram. He felt he had never moved before, felt closer than ever to the actual act of moving.

Stopping at a hanging light with a red glow, Samuel again tapped his fingers on the wheel and looked out. Anac glanced around. The gray, block structure across the street was similar to buildings he was used to. Square base and flat roof. But on the corner nearest their truck was a dark house, painted white but with no lights inside or out. This structure was one of the strangest he had ever seen. It was so pointy and un-squared. There were few right angles. It seemed to be a sprawling mess of peaks and passages. His instinct immediately thought this must be a house of The Order. They were the only ones who built such things. But could there really be an Order this far back? Surely not. He badly needed information, but the vehicle was crossing the street now under the green glow of an overhead light.

Soon, Samuel turned to cut through a patch of grass. The vehicle stopped, and after a few fumbling seconds Anac asked Samuel how to open the door. Samuel reached over to help, and soon both were out. They crossed the lawn—grass, grass, everywhere, he thought—and climbed three steps onto a wide platform. Samuel opened the unlocked door.

"Wait here. Just a bit."

There were two white chairs on the platform. He sat in one and had a fright as it rocked backward. He thought he was going to fall against the wall or the floor, but the chair stopped itself and sent him swaying forward. The chair repeated the motions, back and forth. He sat and rocked. He froze when he realized the window between the two chairs was open, and he could hear voices from within.

"...a who?" he heard a woman's voice ask.

"Shh. Come in here..." The voices faded.

Samuel returned after what seemed a long while and told him he could come in. The overall shape of the house was rectangular rather than square. The roof was peaked like the letter A and went from the front to the back. The porch was covered by a smaller roof and illuminated by a single light in the center. He stepped into a sitting room—or so Samuel called it, making quiet efforts to give a tour. He felt a bit woozy, as if his legs belonged to another. It was that detached feeling of unreality coming to his aid again. He walked on.

They passed into a narrow hall lined along the left side with floor-to-ceiling bookshelves. Samuel flipped a tiny lever, and a light beamed onto a collection of books, a sight that would have been legendary in Anac's time.

"You like books, too, I see?"

"Where did you get all these?"

"Oh, here and there, along and along. People were giving away most of them."

Anac stared at this marvel. The tour continued through the door-less passage at the end of the hall and into the brightest room yet, at the back of the house. Samuel seemed uneasy as he motioned for him to follow. It must be time to meet the wife, Anac thought. What will she think?

Crossing the threshold, he froze. His breath grew rapid. He saw two things. A woman who was no taller than his chest, and at her feet a creature he had never seen except in pictures—the Dog. It was curled on the floor, huge. It raised its head, tongue hanging out. Anac might as well have been face to face with the fiery breath of a dragon. He turned and ran, back the way he'd entered, and nearly tore the screen door off its hinges as he dove blindly into the night.

"Wait! Anac!" he heard Samuel call. Footsteps thudded on the porch. Samuel was after him, but how could he trust a man married to someone so short, and living with a creature like that? For all he knew, the steps he heard might be those of the Dog. He dared not look back, but ran wildly up the street, not shouting or stumbling. Sprinting. And not to the left, which would have been the road back toward the hospital, but to the right, which led who knew where?

An occasional wooden pole light, and here and there a porch light, dimly illuminated his way. Once, he was almost hit by a car crossing from a side street. That was the only vehicle. There were people walking, several of them, and then several more. Some tall and some short. This society was mixed, and his mind reeled at the thought. Whom could he trust or turn to? He channeled his panic into his legs, and so left Samuel far behind.

His muscles felt loose, and he nearly ran over a man pushing a metal buggy. After this he stopped sprinting and walked, again looking back to check his pursuer. Samuel was not there, though six or seven pairs of eyes stared at him. Unmoving strangers. His stomach told him to get away. He walked on.

The houses did not look the same as they had. Some were long and narrow, with wheels under the doors. The bushes and yards grew high, sometimes covering the windows. He pinched his nose to fight a sneeze. Fire had gutted one house, and several more had roofs caved in and yellow tape across the porches. Up ahead to the right of the street he saw two houses that dwarfed all the others. The bushes were high, but the houses rose far higher. A light was on in the upper story of the first, shining dimly onto the high porch. The second house was dark.

He paused to think. A loud noise was blaring on the other side of the road, apparently coming from somewhere down the hill. That was when the barking started. Three black forms on the porch of the largest house rose with the jangling of murderous chains. They did not run, but instead looked right at him and growled. His chest tightened and he stepped back, scared to run and scared not to. He glanced around as he continued to step back, and back, and back. Looking down the hill in the direction of the blaring, he saw a small green building, low with a black roof, and just outside the front door stood five or so people. Some looked at him and some did not seem to notice. But what he mainly saw—with immeasurable gratitude—was their height. All were tall.

He made a break for the group, and the Dogs went wild on the porch behind him. He knew they must be charging for him. The crowd seemed awestruck as he ran through them. One large man by the door grabbed as he swept past. Momentum broke him free from the grab, and he tumbled into a dark room that glowed purple on one side and flashed blinding white strobes on the other. The noise was nearly as loud as the battlefield. People flooded in the door after him. Not everyone in this room was tall. They glared at him. Then the noise stopped, and all went silent. The movement—everyone had been moving and bouncing in all directions—stopped with the sound. The flashing light kept going in a sort of visual contrast to the stillness of all else. He regretted seeking refuge here, but to escape this new danger meant diving into the mouths of the Dogs outside.

The crowd parted as the man who had grabbed for him at the door approached. The look on his face was cold and hard. He walked right up to Anac.

"What in the—"

A voice from the door interrupted. Haloed by light from outside was the figure of Samuel, breathing hard and still wearing the same gray uniform as before.

The room seemed to take a breath, during which the flashing light cut off. Three rows of long and narrow bulbs hanging overhead came to life, lighting the whole scene. There was an odd change of atmosphere brought on by this wash of light. Anac felt naked and transparent. Oddly, a rising sense of intrusion and injustice shook him. He suddenly felt more fed up than afraid, and the change surprised him. He'd been torn from his son. What more could these men do?

The faces of the others in the room mostly showed confusion couched behind hardened expressions. The large man stared at the doorway. A group of women with long, ropy hair huddled just to his left, leaning in and whispering to one another. Four men had been dancing with four girls when the music stopped. The girls moved back toward a wall that glowed an odd green. The men did not move, but three of them held their hands in their jacket pockets and kept their eyes on Anac.

The large man broke the silence. He said to Samuel, "Most folks wouldn't come in here wearing that."

"A. J.," Samuel replied, unmoving, "A. J., I'm so sorry. I'm so sorry. He's with me. This is all a mistake. He needs help. I am so sorry."

The doorman looked at his feet with a chuckle and then looked back at Samuel. "Well, you always do surprise. You can sure-enough have him, but I think y'all better go."

"Thanks A. J."

# Chapter 19

Herson stared at the closed door of Transport Room 502 and thought back to his early days, fresh out of the Academy. He was a sentinel then. What progress—from ditch duty to this, a recovery mission, and of a sort without precedent. A journey to the past, so much glory.

The operation of a recovery team hinged on the delivery of an Auto-Tracc. Each of the three agents on a mission would get one Auto-Tracc, and when a subject was located, a single Tracc could be used to transport both the fugitive and the agent back to 2869. One Auto-Tracc could transport up to five people, so with a team of three agents, there were more than enough Traccs to get everyone home. Auto-Traccs, though, required supplemental energy. Finding a power source was usually not a problem. Yeeton, or enough of its residue, was readily available any time after 2642. The pre-2642 past, though, created a difficulty. Headquarters research published in *The Bulletin* asserted that certain archaic power sources could theoretically provide the energy needed to operate an Auto-Tracc. Core-grane of the $23^{rd}$ and $24^{th}$ centuries was potentially usable. Fission-rings of the $22^{nd}$ seemed possible. But most compatible of all, said the speculative research, was the electricity of the $20^{th}$ and $21^{st}$ centuries.

Headquarters briefly dedicated some effort to the construction of Free-Traccs, devices that could jump time without supplemental power. However, the Free-Tracc project was poorly funded and, in President Leeson's mind, a waste of time. Researchers eventually claimed they had successfully created a self-sufficient device capable of transporting one person, but the results were inconclusive.

After a terrorist attack during the second year of the project, all funding was cut and personnel reassigned to other operations. Agent Herson, then a sentinel at the research complex, had not been on duty when the bomb attack took place, but he was assigned to investigation and cleanup. The perpetrators were never verified. The Order was suspected, but little came of it. Leeson announced his lack of interest in the investigation efforts and called the attack a good reason to be done with a useless enterprise. He did vocalize one lingering concern: three prototypes—untested but possibly functional Free-Traccs—were never recovered.

Herson's thoughts meandered back to the present moment. As he stared at the door, he struggled to overcome a nagging uneasiness. Not the crippling sensation of cowardice, but the anticipatory feeling of a performance that a master wants to play perfectly. The immediate and hurried nature of President Leeson's assignment had rushed Herson's planning. He had been laying the groundwork for years, but had always expected the opportunity to come with more forewarning than this. He'd had only a few moments to stop by his office and get the supplies, and from there even less time to complete the hack of the Transport control board. As he paused before this closed door, he reassessed what he might be forgetting.

A thumping sound broke into his thoughts. The door gaped open and swallowed him into the Transport Room. Parkson and Tagson, strangers to Herson and designated to be his recovery partners, were already seated. No ceremony to such things. Herson took his seat and looked at the two rookies. "Just follow my lead and do exactly as I say."

The attending agent secured the Crane and walked to his dashboard. "You've got forty days. Don't mess this up," he said, with a mixture of conviction and distaste. Then the Transport began—the trademark watering, then gelling, of the air, followed by the aquatic lift to the ceiling.

When the waters receded, Herson was on his feet in a moment and running to the nearest tree. He squatted down. The two cadets were reeling—they had not had as much jump-simulation training as Herson. When they seemed to have gathered their bearings, they staggered over and crouched beside him.

"The first moments are the most dangerous," he reminded them. "Headquarters goes to great lengths to drop us in unpopulated areas, but vacancy is never certain. Keep a sharp eye." Herson was not truly much concerned, but there was a certain obligation to put on a show for these cadets. Plus, he needed to stall before the next jump.

"Did you boys do your homework?" he asked. "Do you know where we are?"

Neither of the rookies replied. Both were surveying the landscape with wide eyes.

"Well!" he pressured.

Tagson whispered, "This should be Corston. Yes. Formerly Georgia. Originally a colony ruled by a king across the sea, once inhabited by a different race of men who were later displaced to the—"

"Save it. I don't need the whole history."

"Should we get a time-reading?" Parkson asked, producing his Auto-Tracc from his pouch.

"No. No need," Herson quickly replied. "Headquarters never misses." He stood, and his two shadows did the same. The three walked slowly ahead and drank in an air none had known before. Even Herson, distracted as he was with the next and most crucial phase of his plan, was moved by this atmosphere. There were no people, and yet, the scattered forest was teeming with life. Everything moved. The towering trees—"Pines," Tagson proudly identified them—were crawling with little gray creatures chasing up and down. The tweet and chirp of birds littered the air, resonating discordantly in the three pairs of ears that had known only silence in the outdoors.

"Tagson," Herson spoke without slowing his pace, "where is your Tracc?"

Tagson answered by producing a black box identical to the one Parkson still carried in his hand.

Herson also produced his Auto-Tracc for the cadets to see. He did not show them the other device, the Tracc of a different sort, hidden in a pouch underneath his vest.

Herson only had to stall nine more minutes. After that his body would be ready for another jump. He knew they were miles from a town, and nothing in this pine forest should betray the actual century they had landed in. He was already thinking ahead to his next landing, knowing his best activity until then was to walk on, saying nothing. This the trio did.

Five minutes left.

More silent steps.

Three minutes.

Parkson sneezed.

Two minutes, and Herson heard it. A sound that was not of nature, and could therefore betray him. A squeak.

The three froze.

Through the towers of bark appeared a snout, then a head, then a hair-covered body, followed by a wooden wagon. Tagson began to breathe heavily. He knew enough to panic.

One minute remained. Herson reached into an opening on the back of his shirt. The wagon stopped, and its sole occupant, the driver, stared back at the eyes that stared at him. Parkson's legs shifted, shuffling the dry needles.

"Where have they sent—"

Herson's Stinger was already out. With two quick shots he stunned both rookies. He had hoped for all this to be done unseen in the seclusion of the woods, but too late for that now. He switched his Stinger to kill, raised it toward the man on the wagon, and fired. The stranger seemed to levitate, as if an invisible bomb had detonated below his feet, or invisible strings had snatched him toward the sky. He landed headfirst on the ground, smoldering behind the wagon. Herson knew there was no reason to check. The man was dead.

One last precaution seemed prudent. Even though they were useless without electricity, Herson still stooped down to the stunned bodies of the rookies and took their Auto-Traccs. They could see him, he knew, but they could neither speak nor move until the stun set them free. He stowed the Traccs in his vest and took a few steps back. Sufficient time had passed. He could make his next jump now. He considered taking away their Stingers as well, but decided against it. What would it matter? The truly safest option would be to execute them both, but despite the cruelty of his present enterprise, even he could not go against that part of the Code.

From the inner pocket of his vest he produced something the two agents on the ground had never seen—a fully functional Free-Tracc. He held his eye to the pinhole in the corner of the device. The air turned to gel, then thinned to water. Sound grew to a deafening volume and a piercingly high pitch. Herson could tell already that this was going to be different, that this prototype was imperfect. Nothing to be done about that now. The water came. He thought he heard through the blur the voice of Tagson—he could not tell for sure—calling out to him. The blur of light and water and air took over and he could not see. The Free-Tracc had done its job, washing him away from both time and place.

When the waters receded, Herson gasped for breath, his chest painfully heaving in spasms he feared might never end. His sternum felt cracked. He thought he could feel internal bleeding, knew he must be dying, felt he was drowning in blood and water and soil and—

His lungs suddenly sucked in a mighty heave of air. He choked. Vomited. Caught another breath, and another, and another. The worst was over, and he knew that he never wanted to make a jump like that again. If his plan had worked, if he was successfully in an electrical age, all he needed for the journey home was an Auto-Tracc, a much smoother ride.

He could not yet stand. Weak and hurting, he rose to his knees and looked around. It was night, and he had to let his eyes adjust. He looked into the pinhole on his Free-Tracc, a method of determining the current year. His hands shook as he looked up, then back in, then up, then back in. His future depended on the accuracy of this landing.

Taking a deep breath, which smelled simultaneously of fresh air and fresh vomit, Herson looked up from the pinhole and grinned.

"2016," he said, and slumped back on the grass, exhausted.

# Chapter 20

Samuel drove with one hand on the bottom of the wheel. Sometimes, Anac noticed, he had to maneuver his truck to the other side of the road to avoid people walking in the darkness.

"Why did you run away?" he asked.

Anac said nothing. His thoughts were random and unfocused. He seemed more interested in how Samuel's feet worked the floor pedals than on anything practical.

"My wife said it was Tater, our dog."

"How can you live with them around?" Anac mumbled, trying to focus his thoughts. The idea, Dogs, real Dogs, not just nearby but inside the very houses where people lived.

"Aw, Tater's fine," Samuel said, grinning.

"I want to go back now. It can't wait till tomorrow. If my boy is anywhere near those woods and I'm not there—and he's alone. In a place like this. With Dogs and all. We have to go tonight."

Samuel let out a deep breath and seemed to be concentrating heavily on the road straight ahead. He drove slowly through the narrow streets. "Alright," he said after a time, "let's go out there now and look around. I've got some flashlights in the toolbox. We'll call for your boy, beep the horn, whatever we can do. And while we're at it, I'll call Miranda and ask her to take the dog over to her mother's. By the time we get home we'll be exhausted and the dog will be gone and we can all get some sleep."

Anac agreed.

An hour later, Samuel turned the truck off the smooth, black road and onto a narrow, bumpy path leading into tall woods.

"We can call out," Samuel suggested as he lowered both windows.

"Sol!" they yelled. "Sol!" It meant something to Anac—he could hardly articulate what—that Samuel was calling too. That this stranger was, for all appearances, trying.

"Sol!"

"Sol! Sol!"

Samuel pushed a button on the wheel in front of him, and a loud blast came from somewhere in the truck.

The calling and blasting and driving went on until they reached the edge of the trees. The lights shined far ahead to reveal a grassy field that stretched out of sight into the moonlit night. The truck was atop a hill. "That's where you passed out today. That's where I picked you up," Samuel explained, pointing his finger down the embankment ahead. With this, he opened his door and got out of the truck. Anac followed his example. From a silver box in the back of the vehicle Samuel produced two large tubes, one green, the other purple. He handed one to Anac, who was surprised by its weight. He thought the device oddly similar to the rod that had smashed his arm at the Housing Agency. It felt like a weapon, and this somehow reassured him.

"Hit the button on the top there," Samuel said, demonstrating. Anac obeyed, and a beam of light went from the tube and up into the cloudless night sky.

"Let's go," Samuel said, and they began walking down the hill and out into the meadow.

The thickness of the grass, a tangled web growing knee high, made walking difficult. The two continued to call Sol's name as they plodded along. Anac did his calling between sneezes.

Eventually, the light beams touched on shadowy masses ahead, and he knew they were approaching the line of trees. Aside from his panicky flight immediately after his landing, he had never been in a forest. The thought of entering one in a strange land in a strange time, and at night, could only be overcome by the remote possibility that Sol might be cowering in those very woods even now, lost and alone.

"This is about where you came out," Samuel commented as the shadowy towers swallowed them.

"You were watching?" he asked.

Samuel did not reply.

Soon they reached the creek. He flashed his light down into the rocky bottom and remembered his dive across this ditch. Without pausing, Samuel slipped down the red dirt, crossed the muddy bottom, and clawed up the far side. Anac followed.

They were surrounded by woods. He was surprised how directionally disorienting this was. Occasionally, he shined his light back in what felt like the way from which they had come and saw only trees and more trees, identical to what sprawled ahead. The same in all directions. Was that the way back? Samuel would know.

"Sol!" he resumed yelling, as did Samuel.

Then, after more walking and more calling, Samuel stopped at the base of a large tree. He stood staring at the ground, and Anac noticed his expression looked different. They quit calling. Samuel stood staring at the ground. In the stillness of this moment, the night sounds seemed to come alive. The noises had been there all along, Anac realized, but he had hardly noticed them. Loud sounds, pulsing in volume, waning to silence, then rising to fever pitch, then down again. Noises from the trees, it seemed. Perhaps it was the trees themselves—some element of the wild forests that had been lost by man's taming conquest. His light was pointed at the tree beside Samuel.

"You asked me earlier if I had been watching you," Samuel said, slowly.

"Yes."

Anac stared in silence. Samuel's right hand held the green light-tube. His other hand now reached toward his left hip, going for something under his jacket. "I was watching you. I happened to be in the right place to see you the whole time. I was alone there, and I saw." His hand was still in his pocket. "Look, I'm willing to help you, and I have a feeling you need help more than any man ever did, but you will shoot straight with me. Drop this whole amnesia bit and shoot straight."

"What do you mean?"

Samuel looked up for the first time since stopping at this

tree. He looked right into Anac's eyes. "I saw you here when you...when you...*appeared*. I saw what the air did, like it had turned to water. And when it came clear, there you were. I saw it all."

Anac squinted as Samuel shined the light beam right into his face.

"Now suppose you tell me who you are."

# Chapter 21

Herson awoke with a sharp headache. The sun hit hot on his face as he assessed the situation. Though having no prior experience with actual time jumps, he had extensive training—simulations, exercises, endless case studies. He knew the procedures and the pitfalls, which was why he'd sought out this particular spot. Standing up, he walked down the embankment and approached the railroad tracks, a key part of his plan. He verified that the Free-Tracc was still on the silver-slick rail. He stepped to the other rail and checked Parkson's and Tagson's Auto-Traccs. They were still there, unmoved. He did not know how long it would be before a train passed this lonely place here in these thick woods, but he would wait as long as it took. The Traccs must be destroyed. All but one, the one to carry him home—him and a corpse or two.

He returned to the leaf-strewn bank across the ditch from the gravelly railroad bed and sat to think. The reason to keep these extra Traccs was clear enough. It would be good to have a spare, or several spares, should something happen to his own. But he knew better. The Tysar Effect, so much of which was still not understood, would certainly be catalyzed by the presence of Traccs. For this reason, the less Traccs the better. The Free-Tracc especially had to be destroyed. If he showed up in 2869 with that oddity as his vehicle, there would be unpleasant questions. It had served its purpose, he told himself, and in this age of electricity, it held no more special benefits. Anyway, it could only carry one person.

He was tired from his uncomfortable sleep and from his long walk last night through those tightly packed, unorganized woods. The walk had brought him to this rail line, which he knew would be here. He had intensely studied the geography of this place and had planned as many details as were plannable.

He sank back into the leaves, finding a spot where the canopy overhead shaded him from the half-risen sun. He stared at the sky, cloudless and blue. He had seen some blue in the 29th century, but the marvel here was that this sky was litter-less. Not a single Helt. He said it aloud, in whispered wonder, "Not a single Helt." All his life the blueness had been but a backdrop barely breaking through the crowded sky, the thick and endless streaks of the Helt Network flying this way and that.

He again entertained a thought that had grazed him once or twice before. Perhaps Anac's or Sol's corpse could be sent back alone. Perhaps he could live out his days here, marooned, unfindable, a fresh start in a new land. The moment the idea flamed up with any real degree of actuality, a single truth snuffed it out—it would cost him his moment of glory. For agents trained as he had been, such a price was the steepest imaginable. Giving up the moment of glory, particularly the lone hero glory he had crafted with the ditching of the two rookies, would be no less than giving up oxygen, blood, food, water. The stuff of his life. Under the cloudless sky these thoughts swirled within him as he fell asleep, a stranger waiting for a train, anxious to get on with his mission.

The shaking of the earth woke him. He had expected noise, perhaps a painfully loud noise, but had not anticipated such shaking. Accustomed to the weekly earthquakes of the $29^{th}$ century, he awoke with a reflex to seek a safehouse, but then remembered where he was, and knew from the feel of the ground—a shaking too subtle and too steady to be an earthquake—that a train was coming. The noise, steady and rhythmic, grew quickly, and then the black iron beast careened around the bend in the tracks, showing its three-eyed head as it rushed forward. Had he awakened sooner, he would have hidden himself in the trees, but it was too late for that now. He gripped his Stinger, not truly expecting there to be a need, and watched the train. He knew he should watch the three Traccs, make sure they were struck soundly, but not even his disciplined mind could resist staring at a sight this new.

The noise staggered him. He sat up straight on the bank of the ditch, watching and listening to the clankings and roarings and shriekings. Sparks at times flew from under the massive wheels. Train cars of various shapes passed in a blur, some covered with bizarre hieroglyphs he could neither read nor recognize. One by one they passed, and the analogy between trains and Trams struck him. Distantly analogous, sure, but somehow not so distant as he would have guessed. The ancestry was unmistakable even after eight centuries. The last car roared past, and with a gust of wind, the train disappeared around the curve.

He slid down the dirt bank, then up the rocks on the other side to the rails. The Traccs were gone. He searched the gravel on the near side, then the far side, then up the middle between the rails. He repeated, back and forth, wondering with each passing minute if perhaps they had been disintegrated. This, he thought, was unlikely. Perhaps they had lodged on the train somehow and were carried off with it. He was not at all satisfied with this possibility, for he needed reassurance that their destruction had been complete. He ventured down the gravelly hill to the lowest point of the ditch. There were small pools of black water there, and he ran his fingers through the first. The water was cool. Nothing. The second, cool again. And then he felt and pulled out a flattened and scarred Auto-Tracc. Useless now, he thought with a smile. To his amazement, as he again dug in the pool, he found the other Auto-Tracc. It surprised him that both had landed in the same place. Perhaps it had something to do with the Tysar. Further searching disappointed him. The Free-Tracc was not there.

Herson combed the area until dark, hating to give up but equally hating the delay. When finally the sun set into night, he made up his mind to assume the Tracc was successfully demolished, wherever its remains might be. He still had his own Auto-Tracc in his pouch, and he decided to move forward on the assumption that his was the sole surviving device. Therefore, only one other task remained before he could begin his manhunt in earnest. He needed new clothes. His training had stressed this point, the commonality of all times and all ages to put extreme emphasis on clothing. No one expecting to blend in could ignore the power of local apparel. Language barriers could give you away, but those were avoidable by keeping silent. Clothing, though, was a top priority. He began walking up the rail line in the direction the train had gone. He knew this led to the heart of Corston. There he would hopefully find new clothes, some food, and, soon enough, his victims.

# Chapter 22

Anac stared blindly at the beam pointed in his face. It was amazing how the light, so helpful in navigating the dark wood, could take away all his vision when directed into his eyes. He felt it somehow allowed Samuel to see right through him, right into his thoughts. Samuel had seen the landing—what now? His mind grasped for explanations. Cover stories. Ways to talk out of this. Playing the amnesiac was no longer an option. Under the beam of Samuel's flashlight, somehow only one choice seemed useful, or even possible. The truth.

"Samuel, I hardly—"

Then, bizarrely, music started playing. From behind the light beam he heard Samuel's voice. "It's my wife. Don't move. I have to take this."

Anac didn't move.

"Hey, Bear," Samuel's voice came through the light. Then the light lowered, moving out of Anac's eyes. Samuel stood there, the phone to his ear. His facial expression changing.

"What? Wayne County?" he said. "When did they—I mean, what did they say?"

Silence.

"Are you alone?"

Silence.

"Baby, I...yes...alright." Samuel, for the first time since the phone rang, looked up at Anac, though he did not raise the light back to his face. "Spell your boy's name."

"What?"

"I'll explain. Just spell it."

"S-O-L."

"S-O-L," Samuel relayed into the phone.

Silence.

"I don't know either, baby."

Silence.

"I am not leaving you there alone."

Long silence.

"Alright…yes…we're going now. Be careful. I love you." Samuel returned the phone to his pocket and looked to Anac. "We need to go. I'll explain as we walk. Explain what I can anyway—all this, it's beyond me. Let's go."

"Sol! What about Sol? Has someone seen him?"

"No," Samuel said, already walking. "I'm sorry. No."

"But why did you ask me to spell his name?"

"I hardly know what means what. Miranda caught it. I don't know how I missed it, myself. But I haven't read that book in so long. Do you know a man named K. C. Sewell?"

They were nearing the ditch now. "Who?"

"K. C. Sewell. He wrote a book called *The Rupture*. Any of this sound familiar?"

"Never heard of it."

"Well, I have. So has Miranda. We have a copy at home. Some of the stuff I told her back at the house—before you ran from Tater—well, it made her think of the book. I should have thought of it myself."

"What does it matter? What's the book about?"

"I think it's about you."

Anac froze, but Samuel's determined pace never slowed, so he moved along, dry leaves crackling with each step. He could not think of what to say, so Samuel resumed, "It's just this book—it's nonfiction, or supposedly. Published back in the eighties, I think. Some sort of theoretical physics or something. I only heard of the book at all because someone gave me a copy. The chairman of deacons at our church, probably ten years ago or so. He said he knew I didn't usually read science books—which, I mean, I do, but I am more a history man." The talking stopped as they scrambled through the ditch.

"Anyway, he said he thought I'd like it since it was written by a Christian. He'd heard me talk about that Lewis line, the one about needing more books by Christians—anyway, it doesn't matter—he gave me a copy, and after a while I got around to reading it. Miranda read it too." Walking fast, Samuel spoke in heavy breaths. They entered the meadow, with its canopy of endless stars, and climbed the grassy hill that had earlier in the day been crowned with a row of smoking cannons.

"But how is it about me?"

"Well, it's about this event he predicts. Sewell does, I mean. Sometime off in the future. But he's always going into these illustrations. Little hypothetical anecdotes. These are—" Samuel paused his talking but never slowed his stride.

"Are what?"

"Well, it's uncanny. One's about a man being born out of a

tree in the middle of a battle—you hearing me? And another is about a man on another planet looking for his son."

"His son?"

"Yes, a boy named Soul. Spelling is different, S-O-U-L, but still, a homophone."

"What? What else?"

"Well, in one anecdote the man is talking, and, well, if I could write down words that capture your dialect, they would be just the way Lewis, I mean Sewell, wrote it. I mean, it's all more than a coincidence. While you and I were riding out here, Miranda remembered the book, and she was rereading it, was just rereading this peculiar bit about the Wayne County Sheriff's Department. The author is from Darien, next county over. And just as she read that part, there was a knock at the door. Anac, they're there now."

"Who?"

"Four Wayne County deputies. Two hours out of their jurisdiction, at my house in the middle of the night. For no reason. No one's called. Nothing."

"Well, what do they want?"

But they could see the truck now. Samuel was walking faster than ever. He did not reply until they were in the cab and speeding through the woods, headlights bouncing off the thick trunks of trees.

"They told Miranda a high-speed pursuit ended in a wreck not far from our house. The guy ran off on foot, they said, and they were searching all houses. I don't believe a word of that."

"So what are they after?" Anac asked amid the bumping and bouncing of the speeding truck.

"If I had to guess, I'd say they're after you."

# Chapter 23

*That night Samuel did not drive me to his house. He and Miranda had agreed to hide me away at some other place they had—he called it the camp house—near the Ocmulgee River. The ride took about forty-five minutes, which gave me time to do what now seemed unavoidable: tell the truth. The bizarre, impossible-to-believe truth. I dropped any semblance of the amnesiac routine and told it all—it was hard to explain, of course, but one immediate benefit of the conversation was that I could finally ask Samuel about the current year. Anyway, I knew all this would shock him, which I suppose it did, but I did not suspect that the greater shock would be my own. Repeatedly, he kept finishing my sentences, like a sort of prophet. I would be in the middle of some part of the story, like the meeting that night with Knowles, and he would cut in with, "And the guy you'd never seen, he was a spy, right?" Or I would be telling about the Tram ride to Headquarters, and he would interrupt with, "The woman, she vomited, right?" On it went, beyond belief.*

*I marveled that a book like this could exist in 2016. How could it know so much? And how could it be read in an age before time travel and still be called nonfiction? Samuel said it wasn't like that.*

*Time travel was never mentioned, and the book wasn't really about these stories of mine at all. The spy or the vomit or Soul or any of it, they were sideline anecdotes, seemingly minor illustrations that readers tended to forget in light of the larger argument of the book. Plus, they were not perfect matches. Samuel said that my versions gave enough hints that he could draw parallels and make connections, but given only the K. C. Sewell version, there was not enough information to divine what actually happened. I hardly saw how that was possible, seeing how much the book seemed to know about me. He told me it felt strange to him as well, that somehow the book became a wholly new thing once my story shined into it. Samuel called me the book's "Rosetta Stone."*

*I told him I had to have this book. I had to see it for myself. It might be my only clue to finding you. And so it was decided. Samuel would drop me off at the camp house then go home to check on Miranda and see what happened with the deputies. He would then come back the following day to check on me and give me his copy of the book.*

# Chapter 24

Samuel turned off the paved road and onto a rutted gravel path split down the center with knee-high grass. The trail ascended steeply, which seemed out of place in this otherwise flat landscape. The trees that formed the trail's walls were of varied sorts, unlike the more uniform forests surrounding the battlefield. The rear tires of the truck spun with a zipping sound as gravel clanged against the underside. Anac realized his hands were squeezing the cushions of the seat. The truck rose higher with each slide and slip and scrape, though Samuel did not seem to notice. He regularly checked his cell phone on which he was receiving updates from Miranda. The cops had left, and all was calm on her end.

At the peak of the hill, Samuel put both hands on the wheel. Anac had been studying the dark woods to the side, but now he looked ahead, and immediately wished he had not. The trail seemed impassible, a cliff too steep for driving. He rose in his seat and clutched the cushion harder.

"It's alright," Samuel said, not looking at all worried but obviously sensing Anac's uneasiness. "It's a bit of a drop-off, but I've been this way many times."

Samuel guided them down into the darkness of the valley below, brakes squeaking the whole way. As the truck leveled off, along with Anac's heart rate, he saw it—the river. Narrow, muddy, and beautiful, it rolled steadily under the glow of the half moon and the headlights. The moon was the one friend Anac recognized from home, accompanying him even here in this far-off time. And it was wonderfully visible now, not like the fragments allowed through the dense screen of the Helt Network.

Samuel parked the truck underneath a square brown house built on wooden stilts. "We're here," he said.

Holding a flashlight, Anac followed Samuel toward the house, past a small stack of wood. An axe leaned on the pile. They went up a flight of wooden steps that led to the elevated level of the house itself. He could not shake the feeling that he had somehow stepped into a fairy tale. Some sort of waking yet sleeping reality. It was all just too much. Dozens of possible explanations as to how a writer in the 1980s could know the comings and goings of a Temporal Transport victim from 2869 ran parade around his mind, and each seemed as implausible as the next. Clearly K. C. Sewell—if this book was real—must have jumped time at some point, but if so, when? And why? And how could he know those particulars? Anac thought also of recovery teams, the most elite and most lethal of CHRON's agents. Could this be how they operated, somehow? Could Samuel be one of them?

Just as this question hit, the door to the camp house swung open, and Samuel flicked on the lights. The steps and the interior glowed brightly, and they walked inside. No, Anac thought, nothing in this whole business seemed half so sure as Samuel's honesty.

"There's no food here, I'm afraid. We'd had a problem with rats, so we never leave food behind anymore. And no running water. But there's Cokes in the cabinet there," Samuel pointed to a row of tiny doors below a curtained window. "Nothing cold, though, but still, you need to stay hydrated."

"Right. Does anyone else come by this way?"

"Never. Anyone coming up that road who's not me, you better be leery. It never happens. I'll be back sometime tomorrow." He opened the cabinet with the drinks and produced two tiny silver and red cylinders.

"Right," Anac said, taking one cylinder, "tomorrow."

"I hate to rush off, but I've got to get to Miranda. I'm sorry. You'll be alright?"

"I'm fine."

With a popping sound followed by the noise of air escaping, Samuel created a hole in the top of the can. He looked to Anac, who stared confusedly at his own can. "Here," Samuel offered, "take this one." They swapped, and Samuel popped open the other. Anac studied the red lettering printed on the side. C-O-K-E.

"I'm guessing you've never had one of these," Samuel said. "I think you'll like it. I got to go. Stay hydrated, and try not to think about food. I'll be back tomorrow with the Sewell book and plenty to eat. Alright?"

"Alright."

"Alright," and with a wave he was out the door and clumping down the steps to his truck. Anac sat down in a yellow chair in the center of the room with the intention of drinking this strange beverage and continuing to puzzle out the mysteries at hand. The noise of the truck interrupted his thoughts. It sounded different. He went to the door and looked down at Samuel, who was sitting in the driver's seat pounding his hand on the wheel. Anac could make no sense of this scene.

The sound resumed as the truck tried to run, but then all went silent.

More pounding on the wheel.

Then more noise, a grinding sort.

More pounding.

Samuel looked up and saw Anac. "It's this truck," he said, "I think I can get it. It's been doing this for months, off and on."

"It's broken?" Anac asked, not knowing what to say.

"It comes and goes. Hold on." Samuel tried again, only this time the grinding was followed by a loud revving of the engine. When the loudness settled back down, Samuel looked up with a smile. "Got it now. Stay safe. See you tomorrow."

"See you then," he replied. The truck disappeared up the hill, and he returned to the yellow chair. He sank down, exhaling a deep sigh, dead tired. Sleep now, he thought, then deal with the mysteries. But first, a drink.

The initial gulp he almost spit out. It burned his nose badly and made the insides of his cheeks tingle. He wondered how people of this age tolerated such drinks. The second sip went better—he was more prepared, and also he took a smaller amount. Maybe it's not so bad, he thought. He kept on, wanting only to get hydrated before giving in to some much-needed sleep.

However, with each sip he felt a lightening in his head. The sensation went from faint to unmistakable. This was new. There was a strange energy pulsing in him, and his heart was racing as if frightened or excited. Illogically, he felt an optimism far beyond anything he had known since landing in this century. Something he had forgotten began to grow in his memory, and he wondered if the silver cylinders held the 21st-century equivalent to his long lost Lorts? He went to the cabinet for another and chugged it. He went to the porch to urinate, then back to the cabinet for a third. He stacked the empty cans into a pyramid on the carpet beside him. The sensation leveled off long before it grew to any semblance of a Lort. Still, he couldn't ignore how good he felt. "That's enough," he finally said. Time to sleep.

But sleep wouldn't come. His mind was alive. His heart continued its sprinting beats. He began to realize he had made a mistake drinking so many of those things. Hours later, when the sun broke through the trees on the far side of the river, he had worn a track in the carpet pacing around the room. He watched the sunrise through the window and only then began to feel that sleep might be possible. He settled into the bed in the corner of the room, oddly alert and oddly exhausted.

Samuel woke him. "Anac, hey, Anac, I'm back."

He jumped as he awoke, and it took several moments before he gathered his bearings. He looked to the window's bright sunlight. He looked to Samuel. "What day is it?" he asked, wiping his eyes and rising out of the bed, shivering a bit.

"It's the same day. I mean, the next day, you know. I've got food."

Anac smiled. He was hungry. "What about your wife's visitors?"

"Nothing else ever came of it. She said they only stayed ten minutes. I still don't buy their story."

"Oh."

Samuel had brought a set of clothes. Shirt, pants, boots. Anac changed. The next hour was spent with full devotion to two occupations—eating something called barbeque sandwiches, strangely warm, and reading K. C. Sewell's *The Rupture*. After a few pages wrestling with the language, Anac realized it was taking too long. This century's written word gave him considerably more trouble than the spoken. He asked Samuel if he would read aloud to him, and so as the sandwiches and drinks disappeared, Samuel read page after page.

As the book marched on, he realized Samuel had been right. The sidelines, the anecdotal illustrations, the hypotheticals, these were the amazing parts. Tight parallels to his own history, but not so tight as to say anything otherworldly unless a reader went into it knowing his story already. If Sewell had done this subtle weaving purposefully, which he must have, then he was a master.

The food was long gone, and still Samuel read on. He was very patient. Only reading, not interrupting, and always willing to pause and brainstorm when Anac asked a question or pursued some thought out loud. Both were invested in this puzzle. Anac's ear particularly listened for any mention of "Soul." One hour turned to two turned to three, and still he read on.

Unfortunately, Sewell did not write anything about Sol—Soul—beyond what Anac already knew. He was in the scene on the train when the woman vomited (*train*, not Tram, in Sewell's version—Samuel paused to explain "trains" for a bit). Soul was in the chair during the blast. After that, the narratives rarely mentioned him, but mostly focused on Anac—personified in the book as a character named Archie.

The evening sank into night, and they had two chapters left to go. The frequency of the references to Soul or Archie had greatly diminished. There was a paragraph on STP (Standard Temporal Progression), which further validated Sewell's insight, for the term, unknown at present, was common knowledge in the 2800s. The final chapters of the book stuck almost exclusively to its overarching argument, which, to Anac's surprise, seemed wholly irrelevant. Sewell was apparently building a case about the misrepresentation of gravity. He called into question the traditional understanding of gravity pulling toward the center of objects of mass, such as the core of a planet or a sun. *The Rupture* argued that a greater pull comes from a larger mass-less gravitational force that emits its energy from a particular direction in outer space, and that all the lesser gravitational fields—those that give a localized sense of up and down—actually derive their powers not from their own mass but from this larger force outside of themselves. The theory was wholly incompatible with the scientific understandings of the 29th century, and, Samuel confirmed, was equally invalid in the 21st century.

"Sewell seems to think there is an 'up' in space," Samuel said, "which of course there is not." He leaned forward, meditatively, then snapped his head toward the back door. "Did you hear something?"

"What? Just now?"

"Yeah, and also about five minutes ago. But I wasn't sure I heard anything."

"I didn't hear anything," Anac said, still engrossed in the book.

"Okay."

"Read on. How much do you have left?"

"Just one more chapter."

Samuel leaned back in his chair, rubbed his eyes, and then continued reading, through a yawn. "Chapter Eighteen. The Void Power. Instinctively mankind has attributed every one thing to some other thing, and in this instance, instinct is right."

Anac listened as he sipped another Coke.

"One looks at a thief and sees in the act of thievery a moral wrongness. But this one thing prompts a search for a deeper thing, which lands the philosopher in the world of moral codes. Perhaps even to the realm of a moral code giver. Where mankind has erred, however, and most particularly in the realm of theoretical physics, is in assuming that the one thing of *gravity* does not lead to any other, deeper thing. Of course my colleagues dig down far enough to reach the bedrock of the 'physical laws of the universe,' but to argue—as I have done in this book—that the underpinning bedrock of gravity is actually extant outside of and beyond the physical attraction of bodies of mass one to another is an argument not even allowed a seat at the table. This, among other things, is why the Void Power is a misnomer that will likely, and regrettably, be implanted deep in the human psyche during the event I call the Rupture."

"Hard to follow," Anac commented. He drank the last sip from the can and burped. "Sorry, read on."

"A similar phenomenon is observable in the operations of memory. Take again our case of Soul and Archie," here both reader and listener sat up in their chairs. "The supposition that Archie could go on 'born-of-tree,' as we have called it, in the alternate paradigm but with no continued fluctuations of being—that is, no variance of what *is* and *is not* his waking reality—is wholly contingent on the underlying bedrock of his memory. He would not know, for he would not have been told, that anyone born-of-tree into a separate existence would lose his memory on the fortieth day. And without memory, he would be unable to return, or even know there was anywhere else to return to. Of course, if he did know, his expectations of normalcy and consistency would be immediately and irrecoverably shattered."

Samuel read on rapidly, "If one could only speak to such a man! If I could talk to him now off the very pages of this book, I would interrupt his search for Soul—as we have supposed it—and shout to him that his days are numbered! Has it been ten days since the tree? Then I would shout that he has but thirty days left. Thirty days until he knows neither Soul nor self. Now consider the paradigm shift implied in this revelation. And what should a man in such circumstances do? I would advise him to attend to the laws expounded upon in this very book. Beyond that, even, attend to the author who wrote them. My book cover says, and I say now: I live in Darien, Georgia, and have made no secret to my residence nor any obstacle to my visitors. Now this scenario applies to gravity, as readers already see, by—"

But Anac rose and took the book from Samuel. He read silently the last few pages. "It's just back on the gravity business now." He flipped around, reading in silence, and then slammed the book closed and tossed it on the table. "Just the ridiculous gravity business to the end! And on a note like that!" His breathing was heavy, like a man just surfacing after too much time underwater, like a man verging on a panic attack.

"It's alright, take it easy now," Samuel advised, rising to come to Anac's side of the table. "We don't know if any of this is real."

"We know every bit of it is real!" he argued. "The whole business. Sewell's been spot on about everything else—why expect him to err on the forty days thing?" His eyes were watering, then running. "So that's it, forty days and it's all over."

"You don't know that."

"We both know that."

Samuel sat back down, and the two stared with empty faces into the lifeless book in the center of the table.

"Well, we have one thing to go on," Samuel suggested.

"What?" he asked, never raising his head.

"Sewell's own advice. He said if he could talk to you, this is what he'd say. Well, he is talking to you, in a way, and so, well, let's do what he suggests. Let's go find him."

"I don't—" but his thought was cut off by a noise outside. Samuel heard it, too. Something had fallen below the house.

"Listen," Samuel mouthed. Silence. He rose and walked across the room. Reaching the back door, he opened it slowly. The sounds of the night rushed in. The porchlight was off and Samuel did not turn it on, so all was darkness outside.

Dry leaves rustled in front of the truck, underneath the wooden stairs.

Samuel reached into his pocket and produced a flashlight. "Probably just an armadillo, maybe a hog. They get up under the stilts sometimes," Samuel whispered.

The narrow, white beam hit the truck.

Nothing.

They eased down the steps, soundlessly. A strong breeze blew into their faces. Samuel bent over the railing, sweeping the beam underneath the house, then beyond to where the river rolled in its endless moonlit reflection. Then the noise came again, this time from behind the truck, in the direction of the woods. Samuel moved forward. Anac followed, stooping to pick up the axe propped against the woodpile. The two walked on. They reached the shadow line made from the lights from the camp house windows and continued forward, step by step. Samuel reached the truck and placed his hand on the side mirror. He swept the beam to the back woods. He held the light up to the level of his eyes, right against his temple, and shined around again.

"Oh well," he said.

Samuel was two paces in front of Anac. He did not look back as he spoke.

"What was it?" Anac asked, still tense.

"Probably an armadillo or something."

Samuel clicked off the flashlight and turned around. In the same moment, Anac saw the horror. From behind the truck stepped a man carrying a Stinger. Anac tried to scream but could only produce a strange grunt, like a man punched in the stomach without warning. He raised the axe madly, and Samuel spun to see.

The moment may have lasted a half second or a half hour. The figure did not yet have the Stinger raised, and if he intended to use the weapon, he never got the chance. Something burned the air. Anac dropped the axe in pain. He thought maybe he had been hit by some stun feature of the Stinger, but if so, the feeling was wholly different than the muscle-locking pain from his shocks at Headquarters. This pain went straight for the eyes. Then he realized that the stranger was down, clawing his own eyes. If Samuel was affected, he did not show it, but with swift moves grabbed the man by the shirt with both hands and slammed his head against the rear tire of the truck, two hard licks. Samuel tossed the limp body aside and yelled, "Get in!"

He slid across the wide seat and reached for the keys that had been left hanging in the ignition. Through blurred vision, Anac found his way into the truck and slammed the door. Dust and gravel flew. The tail of the truck smashed the cabin's back staircase as they sped away. Samuel also ran over several small trees, and a slim wooden pole that cracked the truck's front windshield before clanging over the roof and falling somewhere off to the side.

Samuel groaned in pain, steering with one hand and

wiping his eyes with the other. "Get that canteen under your seat!" The engine was roaring.

"The what?"

"Water!" Samuel yelled.

Anac fumbled around and pulled out a silver canister.

"Pour it on your eyes," he said. "Quick, then give it here."

He obeyed, drenching his face, shirt, seat. Taking a liberty, he began pouring it on Samuel rather than expecting him to do it and drive at the same time.

The water did not heal, but it helped, a little.

The truck bounced off two or three thick trees but managed to reach the top of the embankment. Soon the tattered and beaten vehicle was on the smooth blacktop speeding along into the deepening night.

"Who was that?" Samuel grunted.

"I don't know," Anac said. "He was from my time."

"How do you know?"

"The Stinger. His weapon," then a thought struck Anac. "Samuel, we left Sewell's book!"

"Never mind the book. If you ask me, we've got thirty-nine days to find the author."

# Chapter 25

*I actually asked Samuel to go back. Can you believe that? Me, who always has an eye for the safest route—the path of least danger. But I wanted that book. Two things made leaving it behind seem impossible. 1) It mentioned you. I knew beyond doubt that this was our story. That somehow Sewell knew us, and therefore he could help. The one tangible link to my lost son was back in the camp house in that book. 2) Sewell's book in the hands of that agent, for an agent he obviously was, could mean trouble. If the book was calling me to Darien, what would keep the agent (or agents) from following the same lead and beating me to Sewell?*

*I also knew enough about CHRON operations, about time jumps, to know that the man carried what they call an Auto-Tracc. Agents use these to get back to their home time. If he were unconscious, I could grab it for myself, perhaps.*

*Samuel, of course, refused to turn around. And this wisely. What match were we for a Stinger? But my raising the point about the agent potentially finding in the book a pointer to Darien sparked an important question. Samuel asked how he found us at the camp house in the first place. I was midway through saying that I didn't*

102

know when I remembered that I did know. Of course I knew. I just had not thought of it, for who cares about a Tracker when those who read its signal are eight hundred years in the future? But with an agent chasing me, suddenly the Tracker, implanted in my foot the night our meeting was raided, became immediately relevant.

I explained all this to Samuel, and we agreed it had to come out.

# Chapter 26

Samuel pulled his battered truck around back of a house and shut it off. Anac got out, and when he shut his door, fragments of broken glass sprinkled onto the ground from his busted side mirror. Samuel led the way to the front door. He lifted his hand to knock and then stopped.

"Anac, you need to understand, this is not at all normal. I mean, I don't know how this is going to go, what they are going to say. I keep thinking of what I would do if I were them, but I really don't know. I just don't know."

"We could leave."

Samuel coughed out a short laugh. "No, I'm not cutting that thing out."

He knocked three times. The house was dark except for the two porchlights flanking the front door. He knocked again, louder. A light flicked on and shined through the front window onto the dark bushes. Soon the door clicked and swung open. A man stood there, framed in the doorway.

"Samuel?" he said.

"Scott, I am so sorry. We need to come in. Please."

Scott did not hesitate or ask for further explanation. He stepped aside and pointed them into the house. At Scott's request, the two sat at a round table in a small room connected to the kitchen. Scott went to get his wife. He soon returned with a woman he introduced as Melanie Harper. Anac recognized her as the nurse from the hospital parking lot. He had been prepared for this visit—Samuel had laid out the plan during the ride from the camp house—but Melanie was taken wholly by surprise.

Samuel spoke before she had a chance to ask anything. "Sit with us, please, both of you, and I'll try to explain." He continued as the two pulled out their chairs, "I'm afraid there isn't much time, so I only hope you will take much of this on faith." The tabletop was empty except for a stack of red folders and some pens in a plastic cup. Samuel pushed the cup with his index finger as he spoke.

"What's wrong with your eyes? And what happened to your truck?" Melanie replied. "I saw it out the window. And why did you park back there?" Her voice was more concerned than accusative. As Samuel had explained to Anac on the ride over, the Harpers were far from strangers. Scott was a deacon at Samuel's church, and the two families had been friends for over a decade.

"I had a bit of a wreck leaving the camp house. I'm afraid I owe my wife a new set of stairs."

"Goodness!"

"Yeah," Samuel pulled on his shirt collar, then laid both hands on the table, folding them, unfolding them.

Anac did not know what to say, so he just sat silent, waiting.

"Look. You just have to trust me. There are some…some people after Anac here, and we know how they are tracking him. We would never have come here, Scott. You have to believe me. I would never have come here if I had anywhere else in the world to go. We need a nurse, and I have no other choice."

Here Anac spoke a line he had rehearsed on the ride over, "I promise if you will do this you will never see me again. None of you will. I don't want to put anyone in danger."

Samuel looked at Anac for a silent moment. "Well, he's at least right that y'all won't see him again. We just need a quick operation, and then we're out of here."

Melanie looked as if she needed a breath and could not take it. Anac noticed her hair, fixed differently than at the hospital. There it had been long and straight, but now it looked a tangled web atop her head. He turned to Scott, who hardly had any hair. A gray half circle went around the edges of his scalp, and in the center was bare skin. He was shorter than her, and his expression did not look at all like Melanie's. Whereas her face was white with fear, Scott seemed more on the verge of laughing.

He did not laugh though, but instead asked in a low voice, "What operation, exactly?"

"We need Melanie to cut into his foot. His right foot. On the sole. He'll need some painkillers, too, I guess. Or something." Samuel's breaths were choppy. "I'm so sorry. I, um—"

"Out with it," Scott said with a smile.

"Anac says there will be a tiny disk near his heel. About the size of a dime. We need it removed."

"It's a sort of locator device," Anac confessed.

"Scott, I am so sorry. I really think there is time. I mean, I think we're okay right now. I wouldn't have come if I—"

Scott silenced him by waving his hand. Without speaking he reached for one of the pens from the cup and also grabbed one of the red folders. He drew a curved line, and then slid the folder to Samuel. With a grin, Samuel looked right back at Scott and said, "Thank you. More than you know, thank you." Anac did not understand any of this, but the results, at least, were obvious. Melanie would do the cutting.

Since the urgency was apparent to all, they wasted no time. Anac was soon lying on a bed of towels thrown over the cold bathroom floor. Melanie gathered some things from the cabinets and from other rooms in the house, while Scott handed him some pills and a glass of water.

"How many should he take?" he asked his wife.

"For this...eight. Yeah, eight."

"One at a time," Samuel added, "and don't chew them."

He obeyed, one by one. It hurt his throat to swallow them, and the sixth lodged painfully for a moment. He thought he might choke, but a gulp of water moved it. He was taking much on faith himself, not knowing what a regimen of $21^{st}$-century pills might do to him.

The bathroom was brightly lit, the floor made of hard squares, and he felt the cold on his back even through the towels. His right boot was off, and an ice pack was held tightly against his sole by a brown belt. He stared at a pattern of flowers that bordered the ceiling and tried not to think.

Melanie returned. She held a silver knife in one gloved hand and a clear plastic bottle in the other.

"Those pills need more time to kick in," she said to the group.

Samuel looked at Anac and then toward the dark window. "How long?"

"No," Anac interrupted, "there's no time. Let's get it done."

"I'm ready if you are," Melanie replied with a deep breath. "Authentic Civil War style, huh Samuel?"

"I better go peek out the windows," Samuel said, "Scott, you can stay here. I'm sure all is well."

With that, Samuel left the room. Anac saw Melanie wink at her husband. Then she said to Anac, "He can't stand blood."

"Never could," Scott laughed.

"Alright, all set, here we go."

"It will be near the heel," Anac reminded. "Not on top of the heel, but just in front. You'll see a small mark."

"Okay. You know I've never done this before. But I'll do my best. I am so sorry I don't have more for the pain."

"It has to be done."

Scott sat on the edge of the bathtub and offered him a rag. "Put this between your teeth," he instructed. "It helps to have something to bite down on."

Anac noticed Scott's hand shaking as he offered the rag. Melanie, though, seemed calm. Her fingers were solid as they removed the ice and twirled the scalpel into position. She knelt at his feet and poured liquid from the bottle onto the sole of his right foot. He could hardly feel it against the iced numbness. It had a powerful smell. She then wiped his foot with a cloth, felt all over the lower half of his sole with her thumb, and applied more liquid.

She moved to a seated position, legs crossed, and held his ankle on a towel in her lap. "You're doing great," she said in a soft monotone, her voice amazingly reassuring. He bit softly on the rag and counted the flowers on the wall. One red. One blue. Two yellow. One red. One blue. Two yellow. One— then the pain. A razor sharp, hot pain, as if the scalpel had been heated red before the cut. A clean pain, a deceitful hint of painlessness at first. It was horrible.

"It's okay, you're doing great, it's okay, the worst is over, it's alright," Melanie cooed, endlessly.

He knew now the importance of the rag. Scott said nothing, but he held Anac's hand in a tight grip, and stared at the sliced foot.

"It's okay, you're doing great. I'm touching the disk. Never seen anything like this before. Just need to cut it loose, I think. It's okay, you're doing—"

Melanie was interrupted by a sound—a knock at the door. Though the knocking made Anac flinch, Melanie was careful with the scalpel and did not graze any skin. He was thankful to be in such confident hands, and was simultaneously terrified about what might be at the door. He could not picture CHRON agents knocking, though local authorities might. He thought of the Wayne County folks at Miranda's.

He raised his head. Through the passage he could see Samuel's shadow on the far wall of the living room.

"Stay here," Scott whispered.

Anac sat up, careful not to move his leg, and watched Scott slip over toward Samuel's shadow, which was inching nearer to the door. Both men stood at the entrance, looking at each other, then at the handle. If they said anything to one another, Anac was too far away to hear. Scott stepped over to the corner and picked up a long, slender object.

The knocking came again, sharper this time. Anac and Melanie stared into the dark living room. The knock came a third time, two loud hits. Samuel reached forward to the doorknob. There was a click, a quick squeak, and the door flung open. Anac observed all this from his place on the bathroom floor.

"Gracious, boy! Who answers the door with a baseball bat? What sort of neighborhood do you think this is?"

Melanie released a long-held breath and started to laugh. "My goodness. Mrs. Weatherly. She never disappoints."

"Who?" Anac asked, rattled and relieved.

"Our neighbor. Our nosey neighbor. She keeps an eye on the whole block. Probably wants the scoop on Samuel's wrecked truck. Does that woman ever sleep? Well, hopefully they can give her a story and she'll be off. Gave me a scare though, how about you? Now you just lie on back now. Here, take your rag, you're doing great. It's okay." And she was cutting again as he stared at the flowers.

By the time Samuel and Scott made it back to the bathroom—both smiling—Anac's foot was wrapped in white tape. He sat on the edge of the tub. Next to him was a disk giving off a faint light and changing colors, from red to blue to green and around again, in slow pulses.

# Chapter 27

"We've got to get rid of that thing," Anac said.

"I—" Melanie started.

"It's got to go." He painfully and resolutely slipped on his shoe, the boot Samuel had given him, over his bandaged foot.

"He's right," Samuel agreed, "let's get going."

"It'll hurt him to walk," Melanie advised.

"I'm fine," he said, standing up, weight on one leg, "I—" he stopped, reached down, picked up the Tracker, and stared at it. His mind was busy.

"What is it?" Samuel asked. "Let's get going."

"Yeah," then he stepped his full weight onto his right foot and with an exaggerated cry collapsed to the floor.

"I'm telling you," Melanie said.

"Samuel," he said as Scott helped him up, "I can't. It's not just the pain, I feel—I don't feel well. Must be the pills. I don't know. I'll be better soon. Go toss it and come back to get me. I'll be ready then."

"Let him stay," Melanie agreed. "Go do what you got to do, and he can rest on the couch."

"Can't delay," Anac pressured.

"Alright, give it here."

He handed the disk to Samuel.

"Throw it on something that moves," Scott suggested.

"Semi-truck at the service station or something. It'll be in Kansas before you know it."

"Good point," Samuel said. "Alright, I'm going. I'll find something."

"You can't take your truck," Scott said. "You're begging to get pulled over in that wreck." Then with a smile, "No offense, of course."

Samuel smiled and nodded.

"Take our car. Get rid of the disk, and go check on your wife, too. We're fine here. Come back when you're ready, and maybe y'all can get up a plan then." Scott left the bathroom and returned in a moment with a set of keys that he handed to Samuel. "We won't need to go anywhere, but just in case, leave your truck keys. We just got the one car."

"Right, they're in the truck," he said. Then to Anac, "You sure about this?"

Anac's thoughts raced away in new directions. The mention of the truck keys was a welcome surprise. Finally he responded, "Yeah. Be safe."

Samuel turned to go, then stopped. "Scott, do you happen to—this is going to sound sort of random—do you have a copy of that book, *The Rupture*? You know, the K. C. Sewell book?"

"You've got my copy."

"Right. Yeah. I guess you don't have another. We could really use a copy tonight."

"Why? No, no, don't explain. It's not the oddest request you've made," Scott chuckled. "There used to be a copy at the church, in the library. That key there," he pointed to the ring of keys in Samuel's hand, "the one with the fish on it, that'll get you in the side door, by the pastor's office."

"Thanks. Alright, I'm gone," and with no further discussion Samuel was out the front door.

Anac wasted no time. "I feel," he said, shakily, "I don't—" and he caved to his knees.

"He needs to lie down," Melanie said. "Enough excitement for one night. Help me." And she and Scott took him under the arms and led him to the couch. Melanie brought a large glass of water and a small green bucket. She placed both on the floor next to him. "Drink a lot. The tub's in case you feel nauseous." She also produced a blanket from a wooden chest next to the sofa. She covered him carefully and kindly. "It's late," she said. "Sleep. And take those boots off."

"I will. Thank you for this—for everything. I'll just leave them on a bit more, please. It hurt so much to get that one on."

"I understand," Melanie said. Then she pulled another blanket from the chest and spread it under the boots. "Don't be getting my couch dirty," she grinned. "Goodnight."

"Melanie," he said, looking to see that Scott was out of the room, "have you ever heard of Darien? It's a town, I think."

"Darien? Yeah, that's a little town on the coast. Why?"

"How would I get there?"

"It's easy from here. Are you familiar with this area?"

He shook his head no.

"Well, if you can just find 341, the rest is pretty easy."

"Three-forty-one?"

"It's the four-lane highway coming out of Hawkinsville.

Goes all the way to Brunswick, which is just a bit south of Darien." She went on to explain the turns and signs, red lights and intersections, landmarks and notable features that led to 341. Anac threw in questions to keep her going. She finally concluded with, "Really, there's plenty of signs to reassure you."

"Three-forty-one?"

"Yup. Now sleep."

"Yeah. Sleep."

"Goodnight."

"Thank you."

Melanie flicked off the lights as she left the room. The house was dark except for one sliver of light under the door to the room Melanie had entered. He stared at this and waited. The waiting was dangerous, for it gave his misgivings time to swell. Melanie and Scott were essentially strangers to him, and Samuel little more than that, but the connection he felt here, the warmth he sensed among them, was strong. To leave this behind, to again be alone in the wilds of a long-distant century, was a hard move. Something like logic even rose up to squelch his initial resolve. *Samuel knows the roads. I won't be able to navigate this place on my own. I don't even know how to operate that machine in the yard. I've seen it done but never done it. Plus, I could really use that Sewell book. Wait till Samuel gets back with the new copy. Wait.*

The whole argument hinged on that one word. Wait. Just wait. Delay. To say "give it up" would have been too strong, but "wait" felt lighter, more doable, less cowardly.

The glow beneath the door went dark. The house was down for the night.

For a moment he did not move, did not know if he would ever move. *Wait.*

Then he thought of CHRON, of the tearing away from his wife, of their powers and his losses, of the agent at the cabin. He could never bring on these people, on Samuel and Melanie and Scott, what had been brought on him. He would find Sol on his own, the danger all his own. He could do it. *I can do it. Thirty-nine days left, I need to do it, now. Now.*

Wait.

Now.

Wait.

He was up and walking before he really knew he had made a choice. He opened the door and stepped outside. Silence. He closed it and crossed the yard. His foot was hurting but not nearly so bad as he had pretended. He went to the back of the house. The truck door creaked as he pulled it, so he froze. He opened it some more, slowly. The creaking seemed louder. Then, with one jerk, he snapped it wide and jumped in. Thankfully, the keys were in the hole next to the wheel. He left the door open, resolving to close it after getting away from the house. He studied the mechanisms for a moment, picturing what he'd observed Samuel doing in this seat, and turned the key.

Rrggg. Stop. Silence.

Rrggg. Rrggg. Rrggg. Silence.

He wondered if he was doing everything right. Perhaps the

truck was just malfunctioning as it had earlier at the cabin. He studied the panel some more. Samuel had touched some of these buttons, he remembered. Maybe that was the problem. He punched and flipped aimlessly. He read the buttons before he hit them but could not make sense of what was what. BASS. VOLUME. CARGO LIGHT. Nothing did anything. He hit PWR and a deafening blare erupted. Loud shoutings and strange shrieks. He hit it again, hard, and all went silent. He was breathing rapidly. Then his breath stopped as he saw the window at the back of the house light up.

He slammed the door and turned the key hard, holding it forward.

Rrrrrggggggggggggg. Then, life. The engine fired and ran. He followed Samuel's routine. Left pedal, pull down the lever next to the wheel, right pedal. The truck shot forward as the house's flood lights came on and washed the back yard in a glow.

"Hey!" he heard Scott yell, but that was all. He pressed his right foot down—too hard. The engine whined high. Unfamiliar with such a machine, he jerked the wheel this way and that, knocking down a line of poles in the back yard and spinning loose in a way that felt to him very much like being out of control. The truck shot out of the front yard and onto the road. He snatched the wheel to the right, cringing at a loud screeching sound. Then there came a terrible smell. He had to keep going and just hope the truck would too. Repeating Melanie's directions over and over in his mind, he sped off into the night.

# Chapter 28

DAY 8

*I remember well my relief at being free of the Tracker. I felt that Melanie had in a few strokes of the knife saved my very life from the CHRONs. I could flee now, and not be easily followed. Two thoughts plagued me. 1) I had unfairly ditched Samuel, my greatest ally. Worse still, he had the Tracker. I hoped beyond hope that he would rid himself of it before the agent made it back to town. I comforted myself with the thought that I had run from Samuel to protect him, for his own good. And perhaps the agent had been killed by that blow against the tire. 2) If the agent was alive, he now might have Sewell's book, supposing he knew enough to give it any attention. This thought choked me. Tracker or no Tracker, with that book he might guess I would be heading to Darien. Him waiting on me there might be the only reward for all my troubles. A burning of my one bridge to you.*

*What else could I do? I drove on. The truck, I noticed, sounded different—louder and higher—than it had when Samuel drove. Plus, I couldn't get the speed Samuel had. I knew no way to fix it, so on I went.*

*I was on 341 before sunrise. As Melanie had predicted, the signs reassured me.*

*Except for the loud engine, all was well as I roared down the highway into the rising sun. My hope began to strengthen. Thirty-eight days until my memory would wipe, and it seemed I might make it to Darien before the next sunset! K. C. Sewell was my only chance for help, and with each passing moment my desire to find him grew. A faint candle in this darkness was well worth pursuing, for a faint candle was all I had. Or so I thought. Then it happened.*

# Chapter 29

As the morning grew older, the traffic grew thicker. Anac came to a stretch of road flanked on both sides not by trees—it had been all trees so far—but buildings. In front of him, cars were glowing red and stopping. He slowed, leaving plenty of room, not at all confident in his skill with the foot pedals. The truck was nearly at a complete stop when, to his horror, it went silent. The roar had dimmed to a rumble as he slowed, but then clipped suddenly to nothing. Samuel's truck had somehow died.

He looked behind him and saw several cars drawing near. Using the last of his momentum, he guided the truck to the right and rolled onto the grass. The wheel, he noticed, was now hard to turn.

Safely out of the way of approaching traffic, he tried to restart the engine. What exactly had done the trick in Scott's yard, he did not know, so he tried it all. But something was wrong for sure. Nothing did anything. The green glowing light above the panel was all black. The beep he had grown accustomed to with the turn of the key was absent. No matter how he tried—forward, backward, lever up, lever down—the truck made no noise at all. After a blind and desperate battle, he finally gave up.

He wondered if any of the passing people could help, or

maybe some folks in the town. He wondered how far Darien was. He decided to walk. Maybe some helpful someone would cross his path, but in the meantime, at least every walking step would be taking him closer to Sewell. He could not be still. Sol needed him.

He searched the truck but found few provisions—no food, no extra clothes—only a nearly empty canteen that he went ahead and gulped down. Also a knife beneath the seat, the blade wrapped in a leather pouch. He put this in his pants pocket and headed toward the sun.

The truck faded from view behind him. Then the town faded, and the cars on the road grew sparser. No one stopped to talk to him. His foot throbbed as he limped on.

His mind replayed the scene in Scott's yard. The guilt was a heavy pack on his shoulders. Samuel and Scott did not deserve to be treated that way, but it had been necessary. This he told himself over and over.

He counted the houses as he walked. He had passed eighteen since exiting the town. All isolated, none near another. Some were tall, some low and long, and one strange structure had a metal apparatus built atop it. It looked like a boat attached to a giant fish. A primitive religion, perhaps.

He also studied every sign he passed. There were so many.

341

55MPH

Soft Shoulder

65MPH

Derick for Sheriff

Jesup 90

Antioch Church 3mi

Many held no meaning for him. Others, more self-explanatory, displayed symbols rather than words. These people, he thought, seemed preoccupied with how the road curves. Every turn and junction announced ahead of time by yellow diamonds with wide, black symbols.

The sun was nearly straight above when he reached a large wooden sign surrounded by dead flowers and tall grass that sloped away into a water-filled ditch: WELCOME TO WESTEND. Town names meant nothing to him. However, ten paces past this first marker stood a second sign, a green one: BRUNSWICK 125 MILES. He had learned enough from his talks with Samuel to know, roughly, what a mile was. Here he'd finally found a sign indicating a town he recognized, but it listed an impossible distance. How long would it take him to walk one hundred miles? And could he even do it on an injured foot?

Maybe someone would pick him up, give him a ride, save his life. Another Samuel.

Maybe no one cared.

He rested beneath the green sign, sitting with his legs crossed and his arms limp. Cars passed occasionally but never slowed. He lost track of how long he sat there. The only time he counted was thirty-eight. Over and again, thirty-eight days. He could see the numerals floating in his vision when he closed his eyes. He wept.

For the first time on his hike, he began to talk aloud. "Sol. Sol. Sol. Sol." Mumbles uttered to no one as his body swayed left and right in pointless rhythm. "Rachel. I love you. Rachel. Rachel. Love me. Help me. Help Sol." It was a true break-down. The fit grew deeper until it degraded to a point he was ashamed to face. An old burden, one he thought he'd left eight centuries in the future. He began to dig in his pockets— illogically, he knew. He felt the knife but nothing else. He blinked hard several times. The era and the century and the miles and the pain all gave way to hard, mindless cravings for a Lort. He'd trade all he had—his journey, his quest, his son and soul—for one now. This he thought, if such raving appetites could be called thinking, and he hated himself for it. His chest felt hollow.

He stood in a tear-streaked fit and attacked the metallic sign. He bloodied his knuckles punching it and scraped his palms shaking it. The pole loosened in the soft ground, so he pulled and pushed and shook and scraped all the harder. When he uprooted the whole assembly, he slung it into the ditch. It splashed in the black water and sank as far as it could. Strangely, the physical exertion made him feel notice-ably better. He yanked his sleeve across his cheeks, drying his face and eyes. "Westend," he said aloud, "you'd better have something for me."

He walked on. Fifty paces beyond the sign, small white pathways flanked both sides of the road. Cars had been pass-ing him intermittently for several hours now, so he stepped up onto the left-side walkway to avoid traffic. Above his head, unlit lamps extended from wooden poles. They were identical to those that shined on the street by Samuel's house.

He looked into the windows of buildings as he walked. He observed the cars, many more now, bustling here and there, turning into a drive, out of a drive. There were no other walkers. Aside from the pain on the sole of his right foot, his legs felt good. Maybe one hundred miles was doable, if he could get water and food. He had never walked that far in his life, but his motivation for this trek could not be greater. Sewell, Sol, Rachel. He would get to Darien. *Thirty-eight days, thirty-eight, thirty-eight.*

Seeing so many people in one place reawakened another fear that had, in his preoccupation with all else, gone dormant. His eyes began scanning for anyone with a head injury, anyone with a Stinger. He supposed the rest of his time in this century would be cursed by such paranoia. Maybe Samuel was wrong—maybe they should have gone back to the camp house, taken the fight to CHRON. Maybe stealing the Tracc from the agent was the better plan, the only real plan. Had he and Samuel not been in such a panic at the cabin, they might have at least searched his pockets before speeding away into the night. He stopped and stared blankly into a darkly tinted store window. Maybe he should have kept the Tracker after Melanie removed it. He could have set up some sort of ambush. When the agent, or agents, came snooping around, he could have jumped them, taken them by surprise, taken their Traccs.

He wished he had Sewell's book. Reading it somehow comforted him. Though the book was paper and ink, the hope it held was real, and reading it did something inside him. He tried to remember why, exactly, but his thoughts were jumbling. He shook his head and ran his hand through his hair. Somehow, he could not seem to recall what Sewell had written. How could the words that meant so much not have found a place in his memory?

"You awake, pal?" a voice came from surprisingly close by. Anac jumped slightly and looked.

"Snoozin standin up?" the stranger said with a laugh. The man was seated on a backless wooden bench formed by a plank stretched across two logs. In his left hand he held a knife and in his right a small piece of wood, very light colored, almost white. His feet were surrounded by wood shavings, the pile growing as he continued to slice away at the chunk in his hand. Even as he spoke, he did not look up from his work. He had a thick, gray beard and wore dark brown pants with a red flannel shirt. His head was bare. A hat with a full brim sat to the right of him on the bench. To his left was a flat plastic container divided into thin compartments. Most were filled with small, shiny statues of fish, each fitted with silver hooks. The other compartments were empty.

"You not from around here, are you?" the man asked, still taking slow strokes with his blade—*shewp, shewp, shewp.*

"No."

"Long ride from where you're comin?" *Shewp, shewp.*

Anac was not totally at ease about sharing information, but then again, what would it matter? This man obviously had no connection to CHRON. True, an agent might be in disguise, but this guy was no agent. "A long walk," he finally answered.

"Walk? From where? This town ain't near anything to walk from."

"Corston, well, outside of it. That was where my truck quit."

The man replied with a long, low whistle. Moving his hat

from the bench to his knee, he freed up a space for Anac to sit. "Then take a load off, friend. I imagine you need it."

Anac obeyed.

"Now tell me about your accent. I never heard the likes of that before. You're not from Corston."

"No, I'm from farther off. But I've been staying in Corston."

"Then just decided to walk away?" *Shewp, shewp, shewp.*

"I've got to get to Darien," he said innocently. "How close am I?"

Here the slicing stopped. "You fixin to walk all the way to Darien? Brother, you lost!"

He had feared this. "A long way then?"

"Yup. Long way. Might be quicker for you to get a job, save up and buy another truck. Tortoise and the hare, you know."

"Yes, a truck."

"Or if you want to go old school—and a dinosaur like me is all about it, you know—there is another way. The old-fashioned way." The man leaned in, his hands still paused from their work, his gray beard nearly touching Anac's ear. "Folks used to hop trains, way back when. Free and quick. And the only line in Westend goes right on to Brunswick."

"And trains carry people?" he asked, immediately interested in this potential opportunity to avoid the miles, the impossible miles, racing the thirty-eight days.

"They do when you get on. Now they ain't gone stop the train just for you, let you have a cup of tea and a newspaper, but you can get on just the same."

"How, if they don't stop?"

"Run and jump. Trains through Westend sometimes are smokin along, but more often than not they're slow enough to catch. Specially for a young fella like—" He froze. "Well what do you know about that?" The man reached with his hand to form a cup around his ear. "There's one now." A faint wwwaaaa came from westward. "And it's headed your way, sounds like. And you wanna be sure of that. Brunswick is that way," he pointed east. "Jump the wrong direction and you might end up in Macon."

Anac was already on his feet. "Which way to the tracks?"

"Hold your horses, son," the man said, casually resuming his work. "If it's goin slow enough to catch, you got time. And if it ain't, well it won't matter anyhow." *Shewp, shewp, shewp.* "The tracks are right behind this row of buildings," he pointed with his knife over his shoulder. "The courthouse is back there too, on the near side, to east. You don't want the cops to see you doin what you're doin." *Shewp, shewp.*

Anac looked at the man and then at the building and then up and down the street. "I'm going. It's worth a try. If I miss this one, how long till the next one?"

"They generally come twice a day, but they ain't really all that predictable."

The train whistle blew again, still in the distance, but louder than before. He made a move to go.

"Hey, before you run off, drifter, how about a gift?"

"But I don't have anything," Anac said.

"No, no, son, I want to give you a gift. If anyone's needin help here, it's you, not me. I make lures," the man waved the small item he'd been knifing. "How about one?"

"Lures?"

"Yessir. Just what you needin."

"What are they for?" he asked, impatient to get to the train.

The man laughed in reply, "Well, they good for two things. Fishermen use them for catching fish, and others, well, others use them to feel better. Much better. If you know what I mean."

He didn't.

Wwwwaaaaa!

"For your eye, stranger."

"My eye?"

"Yup. Goes by many names. Some call it, well, you know—a Lort."

He was speechless. How could this man know?

"I see I hit a nerve," the man said, suddenly more serious. "Now that I really got your attention, let me tell you straight."

Wwwwwwwwwwwwaaaaaaaa!

Anac never took his eyes off the old man. His feet tensed. He was ready to run or fight or cry for help, but the man made no threatening move. He only smiled, reached down into a tiny box on the bench, and pulled out two small and colorful fish figurines. Lures, Anac assumed.

"This one here," the man said, raising his left arm, "this one has a Lort inside."

Anac blinked involuntarily. His chest tightened.

"But this one," he held up his right hand, "has what's better. Help for your journey. Help for this road you're walkin. Real help."

Wwwwwwwwwwwwwwwwwaaaaaaaaaaaaa!

"I don't understand," he pleaded. "Who are you? What is this?"

"My name's Mr. Tom Tifforp. You remember that. And you stop tryin to understand and just make the choice you know's right."

Anac felt faint. He stared hard at the Lort lure. Slowly, he made his move for it, his hand raising, reaching.

"Make it quick, son—lookie there." Tifforp pointed over Anac's shoulder to a line of cars on the main road. They were stopped at an intersection, and through the driver-side window of the first, he saw what he hoped never to see—a man with a blackened eye and a bandaged head. The agent from the camp house.

WWWWWWAAAAAAA!

With a swelling in his chest and a choked breath that would not catch, he was snapped out of his dream by the nearness of death and danger. He remembered all that he'd been forgetting in the fog of the Lort. He reached out and took the lure from the man's right hand, then he turned and sprinted in the direction of the tracks.

# Chapter 30

Anac crouched on the backside of the row of buildings, hoping the agent had not seen him. He was well concealed here, unless the car came down one of these side streets that crossed the rail lines.

The tracks were ten paces away, and he watched for the approaching train. The alley was deserted, but to eastward he saw a large brick building whose parking lot was alive with people, several of them in matching blue uniforms. Must be the courthouse Tifforp spoke of. If he hopped the train, he would have to ride right past them.

WWWWWWWWWWWWWAAAAAAAAAAA!

Then, there it was. A large beast lumbering toward him, with glowing white eyes, and piercing, screeching breath. It looked fast, too fast, but he had to try. Staying here was death, and in Darien was life.

He stuffed the lure into his right pocket alongside the knife. He needed both hands free for this. The train's leading edge sped past him. His fear rose because of the sound. Horrid screeches and clatterings and whistles. His ears absorbed the noises as his feet and legs felt the rumblings. The ground shook, reminiscent of the earthquakes back home. He watched as the various containers clanked by. Some were tall and enclosed, the gratings on their sides allowing light to pass through. Some were filled with logs. Some were black and piled to overflowing with what looked like rocks or dirt. Some were flat and empty. One section consisted of nearly a dozen cylindrical cars, like giant pipes capped on both ends. He looked to the side streets. A few vehicles were pulled up to the edge of the tracks, parked beside large flashing red lights. He did not see the agent's car, so he focused all his attention on the train.

He studied places to grab hold. Each car had ladders on the sides and ends. He could try to jump on a side ladder, but he thought it best to wait until the train passed and then chase it from behind. Should he fall, he at least would not get caught under the wheels. Plus, both sides of the tracks were littered with loose gravel, sloping down two or three feet at a sharp angle. Not an ideal surface for running. If he waited until the last car, he could run on the flat space between the two rails.

The front of the train was now out of view, curving to the right on the far side of the courthouse. The rear of the train was still beyond sight. He then noticed that this back alley was no longer deserted. A man in a white cap and white apron was stomping boxes and tossing them into a large green bin. He was only ten paces away. Anac could see the man's mustache and a burning stick between his lips.

The end of the train rounded the curve. It was time. He made for the tracks, crossing a shallow ditch, his hurt foot slipping on the gravel as he went. Over the roar and rumble he heard a shout behind him. Must have been from the man in white. He could not make out what he said, but it didn't matter. The train was gaining speed with every passing moment, or perhaps it just seemed so because he was now right alongside it. He was anxious to jump, but knew he had to wait for that last car. If he grabbed hold without matching the train's speed, the force would rip his arms out of socket.

He readied. The last car shot past. He made his dash, now between the metal rails that ran along the gravelly ground. He sprinted toward a blinking red light hanging on the rear. The light was getting no closer, but no farther either. He was keeping up, but needed to close the distance. His run was troubled by the uneven surface. Large brown timbers crossed endlessly ahead and tripped him. If he fell to the ground, he'd never catch up. His injured foot was splitting pain now. He felt that the wound had opened and imagined the blood that was in his boot. With a final burst, he let his legs burn all they had left. He was nearing the rear ladder, a shot of speed, searing pain. He lunged and took hold of the railing next to the flashing light.

He had it firmly in both hands, the cold steel on his palms. He was latched onto the train but had grabbed too low. His toes dragged along the wood and gravel. He jerked to pick up his feet, wondering how close they were to the razor wheels spinning madly below him. The tops of his boots were scratched and sliced by the rushing ground. He finally got his feet safely onto the lowest rung. He looped his arms around a bar and relaxed. He had caught the train. In this much needed moment of rest, he looked over his right shoulder to see the passing courthouse. His satisfaction was shattered by the sight of many eyes frozen and fastened on him. Among them stood the man with the bandaged head.

# Chapter 31

DAY 6

*When I was seventeen, I rode a Tram seven hours to a training at Homstorm. It was my first long-range trip. The memory of the settlements I saw along the way endured years after. The farther the Tram took me from home, the more unbelievable I found it that people lived out there: so far from anything, so isolated, so alone. Where did they get food? Registrations? Education? By the time the Tram pulled into Homstorm, I was sick—deep in my stomach, akin to homesickness, but not exactly. This was a rootless feeling, as if home, or perhaps the world itself, was not what I had always thought. Of course, all this was before you were born. And I never spoke of it with you, not directly.*

*It sounds strange, I know, but the feeling haunted me ever after, at times quite miserably. I've never heard anyone else speak of it, not the way I felt it, so I guessed (I still guess) it's just me. Your mother saved me from it. Did you know that? She reminded me what home meant. She planted us firmly, gave us roots. Then you joined us, and the unit was complete. A family. A whole. Though that's all over now, Sol, for me at least.*

*Anyway, riding on that shuddering iron beast toward*

*Brunswick, I felt the full force of this same long-lost fear, the old haunting emptiness, back to plague me.*

# Chapter 32

The rushing wind on the speeding train caused Anac to shiver. There was nothing to be done except huddle on the metal platform, as close to the center as possible, letting the walls of the train car block some of the breeze. Still, the gusts swirled and sucked around the corners. He crouched with his back to the wall, facing rearward, watching the trees and gravel recede away in a blur. He hugged his legs and absorbed the bump and sway of the train—strong enough, he initially thought, to toss him over the side.

His fear was debilitating. He felt sure the agent had seen him on the train. He suffered a deep and emotional nausea, raw despair. He was homesick, homeless, marooned. Or was it just the sway of the train that was getting his stomach? Motion, motion, motion, the endless unsettled, nothing like a Tram.

He vomited without moving. The liquid slipped between the grating of the platform and dripped onto the flashing ground below. Then the deeper shivers started, uncontrollable spasms of muscle, not from the cold. He did not know what was happening. He found it hard to keep hold of his legs. The second vomit covered his shins and ran down his boots. He could never get back to his century and he knew it. Who was Sewell, really? What could he possibly offer? He felt he must jump off the train, jump under the train, jump out of this world.

Instead he just sat and tried to squeeze the shakes into remission. The train sped on as he banged his head backward against the cold steel behind him. Banged and banged, heedless and mindless. Earlier, tearing the sign from the ground had calmed his fit, but there was no stopping this one. His breakdown was in full swing when, from the craze, he looked down and saw blood. Something about the sight—dark and wet, splotched across the thigh of his pants—pulled him back to the present moment. It reminded him he was alive. By gradations the spasms subsided, like a river lowering, too gradual to directly notice.

He touched the blood, staining his index and middle fingers crimson. He thought perhaps it came from his vomit, but no, that had hit below his knees. Then he remembered. Extending his legs, he reached into his pocket and tugged on the lure. A sharp stab shot into his thigh. The flood of his breakdown was drained by this physical pain. With a care made difficult by the lurching train, he slowly worked to remove the hooks from where they had lodged into his skin and entangled in the cloth of his pants. He had not realized the sharpness of this strange device. What was the purpose of this thing?

Miles went by during this process, but finally he held the wooden statue in his hand. The two separate hooks had six points total. One of these displayed blood from his thigh— the others were clean silver. Tifforp had said help was on the inside. Who was this man, and how did he know so much? He knew of Lorts, and of the agent. But he could not have been an agent himself.

Anac stared at the lure, wishing for any help this thing might offer. He pulled, twisted, pried—wondering how the inside might be accessed. The spasms of his breakdown had passed, but the shivers of the cold had not. The wetness of the vomit chilled him even more, and his hands shook as he worked. Nothing availed, and in exasperation, he slung the small figurine against the metal flooring. He was making a move to stomp it with his boot when he saw it had broken on impact. Not shattered, but broken in half, a straight and clean cut.

He picked up both halves. One was empty, but the other was stuffed with something white. He removed this wad, a fragment of paper, and held it between his fingers, careful not to let the wind snatch it away. The train blew its whistle, far ahead over the noise of the endless clanking and screeching. Unrolling the paper, he found what must be the help the stranger promised. In this, though, he was disappointed. The scrap was small, no longer than his fingers. One side was blank, and the other held writing that meant nothing to him. How was this any help? His wife and son and home and life slipping away, thirty-eight days until gone forever, and Tifforp gives him a senseless scrap of paper. He placed the two halves of the lure on the grating, saving them. He looked once more at the writing on the slip as the train blew another long whistle ahead. He read the strange markings: ISBN 978-0-578-39886-0.

# Chapter 33

Anac lost track of time. On several stretches, the train slowed. Once, he thought it might stop and wondered if he should get off. But soon the bordering forest blurred again, and the train was back up to speed. A lull in battle, he realized, is a strange thing. Death all around, but still the mind finds space to roam, to think, and even to be bored. He began to count trees. What a century, trees growing abundantly, randomly. His heart missed the straight lines of home, though it simultaneously throbbed in strange reverence for the chaos around him. There is a deep freedom in this land, he thought. One, two, three, four, five—perhaps a thousand trees had passed before he made it to fifty. They passed too quickly for counting. He gave up, started again, dozed in his profound fatigue, snapped awake, counted again. Miles and hours slipped by. His vomit dried and stank.

He must not sleep anymore. He had no way of knowing how long it might be before he reached Brunswick, or where he might end up if he stayed on the train too long. Plus, an agent attack could happen at any moment. He had come to recognize that whenever the train's whistle sounded, a crossing street was soon to follow. Each road, he knew, might hold the black car and the bandaged driver. He thought of Sol, of Rachel, of death, of vigilance. He wondered if he should inspect his bleeding foot. He leaned back against the metal wall of the car, thinking and musing. The rumble below him was rhythmic. Soon he was dreaming, deep and real, of Rachel, of Sol, of home.

He awoke to a pair of faces in a car riding parallel to the train, rolling over a blacktop at exactly his speed. A woman stared at him unblinkingly. The other person, a man in the driver's seat, looked back and forth from him to the road ahead. Anac could not escape the gaze, so he ignored it as best he could. Leaning slightly over the side railing, he looked both directions, up and down the tracks. The road followed the rail line as far as he could see. There were other vehicles on the highway, but they apparently did not notice him. Their varying speeds moved them out of view. Some were faster than the train and sped by, out of sight. Others were dragging behind and soon faded into the distance.

He sat back. He had not thought of the STP since at the camp house when K. C. Sewell's book spoke of it. The sight of the cars brought it back to him. Standard Temporal Progression, a term that never mattered in human history, until it was lost. Before the first Fracture, during the 24th century, everyone knew that humanity was moving along the timeline together, like cargo on the same train. But with the fracturing of the timeline, other options appeared. Suddenly men were being born in the present and dying in the past, scattered to the winds of time so that "past" and "present" and "future" became meaningless words, unusable without the paradigm on which they had always been understood.

All terminology relating to time came to be applied to individuals and not to the mass of mankind. CHRON histories referred to the initial event as the Fracture, but Anac had often thought—and with amazement he saw in Sewell's book the exact same sentiment—that the real "Fracture" was what occurred between people after the event. Isolationism reigned. To each his own timeline, and to each his own way. Whatever else the Chronological Headquarters for the Restoration of Normalcy had done wrong, they at least recognized that life could not persist until men were regulated back onto the same STP, an achievement they solidified in the Great Stand of 2515.

The staring couple on the highway eventually sped on into the future. Other cars came and went, zooming ahead or falling behind. What snapped Anac out of the whirlwind of his thoughts was a lurch and jolt unlike any he had yet felt on this train. He felt sure the beast was stopping.

It slowed over several miles, with periodic jolts accompanied by screeches from below. When the speed was becoming a crawl, the trees disappeared. The train was on a bridge of some sort. Thick, rusting beams rose on both sides. He looked below and saw a wide river of brown water, swirling and gurgling. The height was enough for him to whisper a wish that the train would not stop here, that it would have enough momentum to make the other side. However, with a final jolt, it breathed its last, marooning him mid-bridge.

Options loomed like the rusty metallic architecture. He could stay here, waiting for the train to move on, or he could risk walking on the bridge. He saw water between each of its wooden supports. He wondered if the gaps were wide enough to fall through. And what if the train started moving as he walked alongside? Could he hop back on, or would it knock him over the edge? Perhaps this was just a routine stop. Perhaps the train would press on toward Brunswick in a few moments. Then again, waiting was a trial all its own. The sun was already setting on his third day.

Right or wrong, the fearful height of the bridge won out. He decided to stay on the safety of the train and see what transpired. He did not have to wait long. Sitting silently, eyes mesmerized by the current below, he neither saw nor heard the men until they were upon him, one on each side of the tracks. They had hands on guns on hips, but they did not draw them. Both wore black shirts and tan pants. One wore a large, full-brimmed hat.

Big-hat spoke, "Don't move there friend, don't you move. Now real slow, just let's see them hands. That's right. Raise them up over your head. Thank you. Now you hold them right there." Then to his partner, "Get the cuffs on him, Trey."

"Yessir."

"Mister, don't you know that hopping trains is illegal? And a little out of date if you don't mind me saying so. Where you going?"

At Trey's prompting, Anac rose to his feet. His hands still floated above his head. His thoughts raced through choices and more choices. Words did not come.

"Hurry up, Trey. This train don't stay here long. Talk to us, stranger. Where you from?"

He felt Trey pull one hand down and then another, behind his back. Then Big-hat's face changed. In an instant, it snapped to a fearful expression. He drew his gun and pointed it right at Anac, who reflexively dove down onto the grating, his chest and elbows striking hard against the metal. But Big-hat never shot. Instead, his body convulsed in a strange spasm, like a man hit by an invisible locomotive. He seemed to levitate. Gun and hat flew from him, and in a blink he was gone over the edge and down to the river. Anac heard the splash far below. He heard Trey shriek then snap silent. Rising on his elbows, he saw Trey's corpse. Then he saw the new arrival who had killed these two men. The agent stood beside the train, grinning.

"Found you, 016," he said, holding his Stinger ready, but not pointing it directly at Anac. The agent's face was not terrible or monstrous, not as Anac had imagined. It was just a human face, bruised above the right eye and bandaged beside the bruise. When he spoke, the dialect was pure 29th century.

"It's time for you to go home. I'll provide the Tracc. You should be honored. It's the only one I have left, and I'm sharing it with you. Well, with your corpse anyway."

Anac remained frozen, neither cowering back nor rising up. He just stared and waited.

"One thing," the agent went on, "you are here alone, right? I mean, you haven't met up with your son, have you?"

He wondered what this question might mean. Did CHRON not know where Sol was? "What happened to my son?" he demanded. Then the shot rang out. Loud, too loud—not the sound of a Stinger. It came from up the tracks, somewhere. The agent was hit. He held onto his weapon even as blood splattered from his right shoulder. He folded to his knees, and Anac did not wait for a better chance. He rose and jumped off the platform onto the tracks opposite the agent. Then he made the un-looking leap. Had he looked first, he never could have done it. His gut locked tight as the horrible surrealness of freefall overtook him. The cold water slapped as solid as earth, and the river swallowed him whole, down deep. Then he was thrashing to the surface, taking a gasp of free air, filling his lungs with something that was not death. He kicked off his boots and treaded.

The cold river was nothing to the cold death that had caught him on the bridge. This was life. The air was new, and so was he. Something intangible inside him had been snapped by the hard slap of the water. He could feel it leaking within, a current as real as time. He looked up to the bridge and saw two things simultaneously. Standing on the same platform from which he had just jumped was a man in a black shirt and tan pants—he was pointing at Anac and shouting. Below him, falling from the bridge and then disappearing with a splash, was the agent.

# Chapter 34

Whatever else might accompany this new feeling in Anac's chest, the immediate symptom was a notable lack of fear. An unknown river was rushing him swiftly into a strange and dense forest. An agent—possibly still alive—was somewhere nearby. Local authorities, too, had seen him and would no doubt pursue. These circumstances would normally call him to flee, flee, flee. Now, though, his one desire was to turn and fight. Bootless, he treaded water as the current zipped him past trees and brush growing thick on both banks, but he wanted to press upstream until he met the agent. Find him, kill him, take his Tracc. Whether or not he would use it right away, flashing home to his wife and seeking some $29^{th}$-century means of reaching and saving Sol, he did not know. These questions could wait. A dead agent was all that mattered now.

However, five or six strong strokes upriver showed the strength of the current. He had not known its real force as he went along with the flow, but as soon as he began his resistance, the full weight of the water attacked him. Struggling with rapid and exhausting strokes, he could just hold his position, merely maintaining the same point as referenced by the riverbank. But try as he might, he could make little progress.

This effort would still work, he knew, if the agent drifted at the same pace as the river. They should meet eventually. However, if dead, the agent's body might sink. He wondered if corpses floated. This question was soon overshadowed by the more pressing problem of muscle fatigue. He could not hold his position against this current for long.

He relaxed his arms and let the flow take him. He focused on treading and swimming, keeping regular watch behind him. One option was to swim to the bank, but he figured the authorities would be coming on foot. As ready as he was to grapple with the CHRON, he was not prepared to risk fighting a whole posse. Such a tangle might end his search for Sol. The rushing water seemed his quickest escape route. He looked to the sky and the lowering sun, and resolved to float until dark.

There were dead trees along the bank, fallen from eroded mud, their horizontal trunks half submerged in the river. They reached bare fingers into the swirling water. He stayed mid-channel, not wanting to get snagged and perhaps sucked under by the force of the water. He treaded on, growing tired more quickly than he expected. The woods were quiet—the only sound the gurgling water as it hit up against stumps and limbs.

The river took a sharp bend to the right, and he had to paddle hard to keep himself in the middle. He was a confident swimmer, but his lack of sleep and the time already spent treading were wearing him down quickly. As he stroked toward midriver, he wondered if he should risk a run at the bank. His arms needed a break.

Then he saw a large, wet, brown object just upriver from

him. He thought at first it was the agent—facedown and bob-bing toward him. However, as he stroked nearer, he realized the river was bringing him a big piece of wood. The trunk of some tree, gnarled and twisted on one end and cleanly cut on the other. He grabbed hold, struggled for a moment with the spinning log, then managed to get himself over this round wooden hump. His chest pressed against the topside while his legs and arms hung in the water. This would work, he realized. Not a boat, but better than swimming.

Time and trees passed. The chill of the water sank in. He came to a long straightaway, and far ahead the river bent out of sight to the right. Woods stretched on both sides, far off to the vanishing point, uninterrupted by any sign of civiliza-tion. No house, no tower, nothing. He had little choice but to drift on to wherever this might be taking him. He stroked idly, keeping himself in the center of the river, harvesting the places where the current seemed swiftest. The sun was set-ting and the cold growing. If only that train had not stopped, he might be near Darien by now, nearer to his only possible link to Sol.

Trees and more trees passed, as did muddy water and more muddy water. Birds landed, then flew, then landed again. He heard a mysterious splash or two. Soon it was dusk deepening to darkness. He knew he needed to stop. Night in this water could be dangerous. He dodged the snags and stumps easily now, seeing them ahead in the daylight. At night, though, their only warning would be the soft gurgle of the water striking against them. By the time he heard this, it might be too late.

But where to stop? Interrupting these thoughts, a glow

appeared ahead, its source along the right bank, its reflection bouncing at him from the water, joining the reflection of the stars that were appearing in the pale evening sky. It was a fire. A fire meant people. What sort he could not guess, but his endearment toward the natives of this century had only grown since his first meeting them. Samuel, a true friend already. Scott and Melanie, trustworthy beyond reason. Even Mr. Tifforp, the greatest mystery yet, had offered help. He thought of the strange scrap of paper, now safely tucked in the lure and stored, hooks and all, in his pocket. This reminded him, and touching his right pocket, he felt the knife, still there. At least he wasn't wholly vulnerable as he faced the fire-keepers ahead.

The light grew brighter as he drifted closer. He was surprised how long it took to get noticeably nearer, and wondered if the river had slowed. The sun certainly had not. Before he closed a third of the distance, the darkness was complete. A half moon gave what light it could, the stars aiding in their own way, far more stars than he was used to. His primary means of keeping his bearings was the fire's red-orange glow. He made for it, stroking softly ahead, aiding the current. Closer still and he heard the voices. Watery mumbles at first, then audible. Comprehensible.

"...it ain't like that at all, I told him," one voice went on, high and whiney. An accent unlike Samuel's but not so far removed from Scott's. "And they sent the, I guess you'd call him the revenuer, and went on about dubbya-twos and ten-forties and withholdings till a man can't sell a lawnmower no more."

"Turn that up," a different voice called, a deep boom of

a voice. Then a new noise started, a song with music and words. Something about a train on Tuesday.

"They don't make em like that anymore," the deep voice bellowed over the blaring music.

Anac made for the bank a little upstream from the fire. He thought it better to approach on foot. The current was a standstill near the shore, and he was thankful for this. He grabbed thin, tangly roots as he slipped up the slick mud. Above a short and steep hill the land was level and firm. He walked through the trees in the direction of the fire. Twigs crackled beneath his shoeless feet. He was close, the glow of the fire visible now. He could hear the voices again.

"Your dang CD's skipping."

"Shh."

"What?"

"Shut it."

Then, out of the darkness, a blinding light attacked Anac's eyes, disorienting him. He froze.

"Who's there?"

"What?"

"Pops, turn that dang radio off!"

"Scared off bout every animal in the jungle, I'd say, with all that racket. Y'all don't have no Bill Monroe? No, you wouldn't. You know what I says to him? 'I been selling since before I was born, and more than lawnmowers, and this small change ain't a bit of your concern, and tell that—'"

"Pops, hold on, please, hush a minute."

The light never left Anac. There was no hiding. He considered flight into the jungle, or diving to the ground. But the point of getting out of the water was to meet people, to get help and direction. He was not going to find Darien by himself, not in this wilderness. Only thirty-eight days left—he had to take chances. He stepped toward the light. "Hello!" he called.

"Put that down," one voice said.

"What's the deal, bud?"

Anac walked toward them. The light was still on him, but not right in his eyes. He could see their shadowy outlines now. Two men were standing on some sort of clearing, a low rise that stretched from the water to the woodline.

"Hey," he said, not knowing what to say. "I—uh—I fell in the river. I need some help, please."

"Now that's an accent."

"For sure."

"What's your name?"

"Anac." He entered the clearing, which was all sand. "I fell in. I'm cold. Can I dry off by your fire?"

"Were you in a boat?"

"No, no, I was—" His mind grasped for anything plausible. If he wasn't soaking wet, this would be easier. "I was walking and got lost," he stammered, "and I went so long I got thirsty, and so I stepped to the river for water and slipped on the mud and fell in. It was deep. I had to kick off my boots to swim out."

"Oh."

"I've been walking ever since. I have no idea where my truck is. I just heard your music and saw your fire."

And on like that it went—more questions and more fabrications—as he tried to sound believable. They walked him to the fire and gave him a blanket. All sat. There were three men. The two nearest him seemed more at ease as time passed. The third, sitting in a chair on the other side of the fire, paid no attention to any of this. He talked unceasingly, his high-pitched voice marching on as it had since Anac first came within earshot. "Mowers is it, though. I told y'all over and over, but did they want to put up the money? Nope, nope. But look at it now..."

Anac's teeth chattered. He noticed that one man held a small gun on his thigh, and the other an object not unlike Samuel's flashlights. The area was treeless and dry, a land platform on the inside of a wide curve in the river. The fire crackled and reflected off the swirling waters that had delivered him to these strangers. He saw no vehicle—only the fire, some pots and bags, a pile of wood, stumps standing on end, four tents, and the old man who had still not stopped talking.

"You need some dry clothes, bud," the shorter man said. "You'll see em in that tent." He pointed. "I got some knee waders you can wear too." He then leaned over and picked up a large device Anac did not recognize. He laid it across his lap, and with a flick of his hand, it rang out an eerily pleasant sound.

"Better go change," the taller one coaxed as he worked with some metallic pots near the fire. "I'll have you something warm to eat when you get out. You won't be cold when you're dry. It's just crisp enough to keep the bugs away, but not bad."

A smell was growing, and Anac realized how hungry he was. "Thank you," he said. "I'll go change." And he did.

He emerged from the tent wearing black pants, a blue

button-up shirt, and a puffy green jacket, all fitting surprisingly well. He had transferred the knife and Tifforp's lure from his wet pants to the pockets of this new jacket. The tight-fitting black boots he now wore were rubbery and tall, going up nearly to his knees. He'd removed Melanie's bandage, but had on fresh, dry socks. As he resumed his seat by the fire, he noticed the old man was silently slumped in his chair, asleep. The short man still plucked away at his whatever-it-was. The pulse of the noise was unlike anything Anac had known before. It struck him someplace deep, and deeper still when the taller man handed him a plate of food and a fork. He sat on a log and ate without hesitation, something white and steaming, his hunger overcoming the unusualness of hot food.

His mind kept pace with his fork. What to say to these two? How to go about this? He wondered again if corpses floated. If so, Big-hat might have already come by and these campers simply not seen him. Or was he submerged under the bridge still? And the agent might come floating by any minute. Perhaps the agent was not a corpse at all.

"I'm Ryan," the shorter man said, pausing his playing. "That's Reece."

Reece handed Anac a can much like the Cokes from Samuel's camp house, though these were not quite the same color. Remembering how good those drinks had made him feel, and tasting the dryness of his mouth and throat, he cracked open the lid and took a big swig. It burned his throat. He drank again.

"Let me know if you need some more."

"No more, thanks. Can I hold your flashlight?"

"Sure," Reece said, as he reached for his light. "Just press that button there."

Anac did, aiming the bright beam toward the water. He could see plainly the whole width of the river. He swept upstream and then down, seeing nothing, but noticing on the downriver side of the clearing a narrow boat pulled halfway up on the sand.

"Looking for something?" Ryan asked, playing as he talked.

"No. No, it's nothing." He cut off the light. "Just trying to figure out this place. Where are we, anyway?"

"We're on Grimson's Bar," Ryan said, "eight turns from where the Altamaha starts."

"The Altamaha?"

"You are a lost soul, ain't you?"

His throat tightened at the sound of Sol's name, but then he realized what Ryan had actually said. "I suppose so. I'm sort of new to this area. I guess that's how I got so turned around in the woods."

"Were you hunting?"

They had asked him this before. He wondered why the repeat. "No," he said, "just walking."

"Oh. Well, the Ocmulgee, downriver just a bit it joins with the Oconee and they form the Altamaha."

"So how far are we from Darien? Or have you ever heard of it?"

"Sure," Ryan said, "I've heard of it. It's not too terribly far, once you get on the highway. An hour or two." Then he added, still plucking away, "Of course you could go by boat. This river flows right to Darien. It'd take a while, though."

This was a thought. Traveling by water. It might lead to

capture since the authorities had seen him hit the river, but train riding was out, and he had no other means of transportation except his feet. He was no doubt a long way from 341, and without it, without that simple straight-shot highway, how could he avoid getting lost? Moot point though, for he had no boat, unless he stole Reece and Ryan's. Latching onto another log, continuing his soaking float, was an uninviting option.

"Look," Reece said, opening his own canned drink, "we'll be glad to give you a ride tomorrow morning, help you find your truck. Ours is right over there," he pointed.

"Yeah, for sure," Ryan agreed, now humming as his fingers stroked the strings.

Anac really wanted that boat, but then again, he had no idea how to operate it. Perhaps he could steal their truck.

"That sounds good to me. Thank you both very much."

"Good deal," Reece said, stepping to the woodpile.

Then Ryan began to sing. Anac sat back, his plate now empty, and sipped his drink, which was having an invigorating effect. Occasionally, as the song rolled on, he would sweep the river with the light.

Reece spoke up, " 'Comin Home,' now that's a song." Then he leaned in toward Anac. "If you don't want to sleep under the stars tonight," he said, "you take that tent there." He pointed to the one where Anac had changed clothes. "We just keep supplies in that one. Shove them out the way and there'll be plenty room for you."

"Thank you."

"You like Lynyrd Skynyrd?"

"I, uh—"

But the old man across the fire was awake again. "Dad-blame-it! My back. Y'all done bored me to sleep out here with all your talk. I'm goin to bed." He rose, then tottered over to one of the four tents and zipped himself inside.

The music flowed on, haunting and beautiful.

"And hush that guitar up!"

Ryan obeyed, his instrument and his voice falling silent as he and Reece exchanged a look and a laugh.

"He's right," Reece said. "Time for bed."

Alone in the supply tent, Anac knew it was time to make up his mind. Steal the boat, steal the truck, or wait until morning and take their offered ride. He listened to the night noises, felt his dry clothes and his warm blanket. Deep fatigue decided for him. He laid his head on a soft pack, kicked off his boots, and closed his eyes. He thought of Sol, of Rachel, and of the knife in his hand.

# Chapter 35

He awoke with a jolt, forgetting for a moment where he was, then orienting himself quickly and picking up the knife that he'd dropped as he slept. It was still night, but something was moving. It sounded like shuffling feet on the sand, coming from the direction of the river and getting closer. He noticed too that the red glow of the fire, which had before been visible through the thin walls of his tent, was now gone.

He felt vulnerable. He could see nothing of the goings-on outside. The knife was reassuring in his tight grip, its empty leather sheath in his pocket. He had not lost the thirst to take the offensive, to end this agent. Crouching near the ground, weight on his toes, he readied for his attack. The shuffling drew nearer, then paused. Whoever it was had stopped near the location of the expired fire. In one motion, Anac snatched up the door and leapt, but his sliced foot landed on a stake in the sand, the result being that this otherwise ferocious attack turned into a graceless fall. He got up off the ground, knife in hand.

"Good morning to you too," Reece said, kneeling on the sand next to a red bed of coals.

He relaxed and dropped his knife. At that moment a loud tearing sound let loose behind him. He snatched around and saw the boat backing out into the river. Ryan was in it, a light attached to his head and smoke surrounding his vessel. He continued to back up until he reached the middle of the river. The current was pulling him swiftly down. The engine revved sharper and louder as the boat cut a tight turn and sped off, following the current. The light from his head and the whine from the motor receded into the night and disappeared around a curve.

"He's going to check the limb lines," Reece explained, stuffing something into the coals.

"Limb lines?"

"For catfish. We're sorry fishermen, really. We should have been checking them all night, but we were too tired. Plus, I mean, really, you were more interesting." Smoke began to rise from the pit, and soon Reece was throwing whole logs onto the fire. "Sun'll be up in a bit. We'll get us some breakfast and then I can take you. Pops'll stay here and man the camp."

"To find my truck."

"Yup."

He shifted his feet in the sand, then bent down to pick up the knife, reaching into his pocket for the sheath. He covered the blade and stuffed it in his jacket.

He sat and studied the river as Reece clinked with a pan near the fire. The black sky was turning to gray, and the smell of food grew with the light. He was hungry and cold, but more than that he was anxious to get moving. His thoughts wrestled with the problem of them searching for a truck that was not there. Could he talk his way into a ride to Darien, or at least in Darien's direction? Should he just try to steal their truck now?

"I gotta go," he said, pointing to the woods.

"Yeah. Toilet paper is in your tent if you need it."

He put on his boots, left the toilet paper, and walked toward the woodline. The sand led into a tangle of leaves and twigs, which broke under his feet with the same noise that had given him away last night. A footpath curved through the undergrowth, and he followed it until the truck came into sight, off to the left. He hopped a large fallen log lying between him and the truck, and then he was there, hand on the door, pulling. It would not move. He walked around and tried the other door. Same thing. He tugged on the side windows and then climbed into the truck's bed and pushed on the rear glass. No luck. While pushing, he noticed a symbol painted in the corner of the window. It looked familiar, somehow. He jumped down, relieved himself, and went back to the sandbar.

The brightness of a new day surprised him as he exited the woods. The light had grown quickly. Reece sat next to the fire eating from a black bowl. Anac took a seat next to him and picked up another bowl of steaming food. They ate in silence. When the bowls were empty, Reece collected them and then went on to pour a brown liquid from a kettle into two cups. Anac took one and drank. He did not like its flavor or its heat, but as the sips passed, he recognized the feeling—a rising in the mind, an awakening, like from the Cokes.

"Well, let's go," Reece said. "I'll wake up Pop and you and me'll hit the road."

"Thank you," he said, meaning it.

"Yeah."

The old man seemed another person in the morning. Younger, somehow, in his movements, and he talked far less.

"Good morning there, driftwood," he said to Anac with a laugh. "You going to stay with us today or swim on down the river?"

Reece answered, "I'm going to take him to find his truck. I'll be back soon. Can you watch the fire and take care of your breakfast?"

"I taught you how, didn't I? I'm fine. Y'all go-on," he untipped a chair by the fire and sat down. "Ryan go up or down?"

"Down."

"Smart. Y'all go-on."

Reece stuffed a few items from the cooler into his pockets and led the way to the woodline.

Anac followed. When they reached the truck, he asked about the symbol on the window.

"You don't know what that is?"

"I feel like I've seen it before."

"Hop in."

They slammed their doors and Reece fired up the engine, which roared deeper and louder than Samuel's. The road was dirt, narrow and bumpy. The headlights shined ahead of them, but the dimness in the woods was swiftly dying into daylight. Reece drove faster than Samuel, and he talked steadily as he went.

"So that bumper sticker is the Jesus fish."

"Oh."

"Yeah, Mama put it on my truck. It's just a sign that

someone's a Christian—a believer. It's got a pretty old history, so the story goes."

"A believer in what?"

"You know, in Christ."

"Oh."

The dirt road ended, forming a T-shape with a wider blacktop. Reece pointed, "You came from this way, right?"

Anac nodded.

Reece turned right and drove on, faster than before. "The early Christians needed a way to identify one another in secret, to avoid persecution, you know. And so if two folks met and one wanted the other to know he was a Christian, he'd draw half of the fish in the sand, just one line. A curved line." Reece traced this imaginary shape in the air with his finger. "And if the other guy was a believer too, then he would draw the other line and complete the fish. Then they both knew without anyone else having to know. You see?"

Anac raised his own finger to draw the imaginary line, the half fish, in the air. He recognized it. "I've seen that," he said, "That's what—"

"Whoa!" Reece yelled, snatching the wheel and the truck hard to the left side of the road. "Get your head down! That guy's got a gun!"

Anac snapped his whole body down onto the seat and Reece did the same, only keeping one hand on the wheel and his head just high enough to see over the dash and to the road. The engine roared louder. The back window exploded. Shards of glass covered them both.

"Stay down!" Reece called, peeking up in quick snatches.

But Anac had to look. He risked raising his head enough

to see back through the gaping hole where the glass had been. Wind whipped his face and he squinted his eyes against any pieces of glass that might be flying. The agent was standing in the middle of the road. Reece was silent now, intent only on driving. Glass and wind and noise were everywhere. A minute later and Anac risked another look. The agent was out of sight. The road had curved. "I don't see him anymore," he said.

Reece sat upright, both hands on the wheel now, the truck flying along. "What was that?"

"He's after me," Anac said. "Put me out here, I'm not keeping you in danger. Let me handle this." He felt fear and anger and energy all wrapped up and symbolized in his mind by the shape of his knife blade. He did not want to retreat.

"After you?"

"Stop the truck—let me out."

"Who is he?" The wind was whipping, the engine roaring.

"You wouldn't understand. He's after me, that's all. He wants to kill me. I think they're after my son too. I've got to face him."

"Oh no!" The tires screeched as Reece stomped the brakes and skidded to a stop. A car was coming toward them in the other lane. Reece blared his horn and waved his arm wildly.

"What are you doing?"

"We can't let them go toward that guy!"

The car was close now, slowing down but not stopping. It was a low vehicle, dark green. Reece jumped out and stood in the other lane waving both arms over his head and shouting "STOP! STOP! STOP!" At this, the other car picked up speed. Rather than stop, it seemed intent on getting by. It cut into the grass along the side of the road. With dirt spinning up behind, it shot past Reece who was still waving his arms.

He jumped back in the truck. "I tried," he said. "We gotta put some distance between us and him, and we got to call the cops." The truck lurched forward, engine roaring again.

Reece reached into a compartment on the dash and pulled out a phone. He punched four numbers and soon began to talk, explaining the situation. He said sharply, "Just send em, I got to make another call, send em!" He punched some more numbers and soon was talking again, "Ryan, listen bud, you gotta get back to camp, now, get back to camp and get Pops and get the widow-maker and get down the river, you hear me... Just listen! Someone's after this guy that walked up last night... I know, I know. He shot at us... No, the other guy. My truck's all messed up. We're fine. Get Pops and get down the river. Don't stay at the camp. If I can I'll meet y'all at Morris Landing. Just get there no matter what... Morris Landing. Either I'll meet y'all there or get someone to. I called 911 already. Gotta go. You got it?... A'ight, go."

Reece put the phone in his pocket and sped on, saying nothing to Anac but looking at him from time to time. Anac glanced behind them but saw nothing. The wind-whipped truck raced on.

"Who are you?"

"What?"

"You tell me what's going on or you're about to go flying out of a moving truck."

"That guy is after—" Then he had a sudden idea. "Reece, what would your Pops do to save you, I mean, if you were in danger?"

Reece's jaw tensed.

"That guy back there, he's after my son. He's out to kill him."

Reece put both hands on top of the wheel as he skidded around a sharp bend in the road. His forearms were straining.

"Well?" Anac said, looking alternately at the road behind them and at Reece's face.

"We're just going to drive a while, that's all," Reece declared.

They did. Reece made several turns at blacktop intersections, and soon the road ended at a wide crossroads. It looked familiar. "Is this 341?" Anac asked.

"Yup." Reece turned left and shot off eastward.

Anac checked behind them again. "Reece, Reece, look."

Reece turned. Both men watched as that same green car, the one that had passed them in the ditch, sped into the intersection, swerving and spinning wildly. The car's side window was blown out.

"It's him!" Anac shouted.

"It is," and Reece revved the engine even louder and focused all his attention on driving. "You watch him," he said, "and if he shows that gun you tell me."

The chase was on, and the car was gaining quickly.

"Faster!" Anac said.

"It's fast as I got. Any gun?"

"No, nothing yet."

"What's he doing?"

The car drew so close that he could see the agent's face. Only one of his hands was on the wheel, and he figured he held the Stinger in the other. But why didn't he fire it? Then he realized. "Watch out! He's going to ram us!"

Reece said nothing, but he looked back and cut the wheel to the right, to the left, to the right again, trying to dodge the attacking car. Then they collided, the front of the agent's car striking hard against the back left corner of the truck. A strange and horrid slow motion followed. Reece may have said something, but it was muddled. Trees, road, trees, road, trees, road swirled around. The scene grew even slower, surreal in its pace. Anac felt he had time to open the door and calmly get out. Time to think, to plan, to reflect, to talk— though he could think of nothing to say.

The tires screeched horribly on the asphalt. The deceitful slowness gave up the lie when the truck reached the grass in the median of the highway. They were sideways then, and the truck skidded hard, leaning up on the right two wheels. This was when the speed became full-real. They were flying, racing, blistering along as dirt and grass shot up before them like water. They tilted horribly, Reece's side going high into the air. Somehow the truck did not flip. Catching in the valley of the ditch, everything stopped and the high side of the truck slammed down. There they sat, dazed, as the engine choked off.

Silently stunned, they looked at each other. A reverent moment passed as each realized that neither was hurt. Then Reece kicked open his door and staggered out. Anac did the same. That was when he saw it.

"Run!" he called to Reece.

They took off for the woodline, hoping the trees would provide cover. The green car, front end smashed, was chasing them. It spun wildly and made a leap over the near side of the median. Anac saw this while looking over his shoulder, boots splashing into the ditch that bordered the woods. Twenty paces to reach cover. The car's rear tires squealed as they caught traction on the asphalt. It catapulted forward. The trees were close, but the car was closer. They sprinted madly, no longer bothering to look back. A desperate flight.

Then came a crash, loud and horrible, like trains colliding. Anac snapped his head back and saw that he need run no more. The agent's car was not behind them. It was a good distance up the road, flipped. Tangled with it was a large brown and white vehicle with blue strobes streaking from the roof. A siren blared.

"The police," Reece said, and stopped.

The front of the police car was smashed in. The green car was upside down and folded into itself. Anac figured the agent must be dead.

He stood frozen, both afraid and relieved. It was in this awed state that he saw the cop kick open his crinkled door and stagger to the agent's car. He reached in through the broken window and dragged the body out, grating it over jagged glass. Anac and Reece looked on, paralyzed. A second police car, tall and boxy, raced up and screeched to a stop on the highway above them. This one's lights and sirens were also full blast.

The first deputy propped the agent up against a tire, looked at something beneath the man's collar, and then punched him hard across the face. To Anac's astonishment, the agent was alive. His eyes opened and his head moved a bit.

"My glory, all! What about it?" the cop said. "Where's

your glory now?" Then he reached both hands over a deep, blood-soaked gash in the agent's arm and twisted hard. The half-conscious agent let out a horrid cry. "Where are the Traccs?" the cop yelled.

Reece, unmoving, spoke to Anac, "What is this?"

But before he could answer, a loud, electronic voice came amplified from the second vehicle: "Get in, now! Come on, come on, come on, now!"

They obeyed, running then jumping into the back seat.

"You're safe in here," the driver said.

"What's that guy doing?" Reece demanded.

"Just trust me."

The outside cop pulled his pistol and shot the agent in the head. He then began to rifle through the man's pockets. A new siren blared from up the highway, and the driver in the front seat got on the speaker again. "Time to go, Phillip!" he called.

The one named Phillip immediately gave up his search, ran to the car, and hopped in the front seat. He wore a black uniform identical to the driver's, and his hands were covered in blood.

# Chapter 36

They drove ten minutes at blurring speed, lights flashing, siren blaring. No one spoke. In the back seat, Anac shot several pleading looks at Reece, but received no reply. Reece looked angry. He stared at the floorboard, unmoving, unspeaking. Anac wondered if he was mad at him. The cops up front stared straight ahead. The tires hummed. Then the blue lights went off, and the siren went silent. A hat rested on the dashboard, WAYNE COUNTY SHERIFF written across its face.

"You were in Corston, weren't you?" Anac asked, speaking through a metal cage that separated the rear seat from the front.

"Yes."

"Who are you? What is this?"

"We've been after you since you got here. You're pretty hard to find, for someone who's not local."

"Not local?"

"Drop it. We know all about you, Anac."

The driver made several turns, finally steering the car down a white dirt road. At a narrow spot surrounded by trees on both sides, he stopped. A clamoring noise was rumbling in the woods. The cops got out. When their doors opened, the clamor outside grew louder. Then the front doors slammed.

As the rear doors opened, the clanging outside swelled again. Both men had weapons in their hands. Short, black some-things.

"Out," the one on Reece's side said.

They obeyed, Reece exiting out one door and Anac the other. The cops led them to the rear of the vehicle and instructed them to sit on the narrow bumper. Dark brown water trickled in the ditches. Whatever machine was operating in the woods, it was out of sight, and its noise sounded farther off than Anac had first thought. Reece made no sound. He still looked angry. He might be in shock, Anac thought.

"We need to explain some things to you Anac, but first we need to talk to your friend. This doesn't concern him. It's in your best interest that he buy what we're selling, if you get me."

"I don't get anything. I don't have a clue who you are!"

"We know about Sol."

In a blink, he had drawn the knife from his pocket and pounced on the nearest cop. He knocked him to the ground and had the knife at his throat. He couldn't get it closer, though, because his arm was now caught in a tight grip. The grounded cop had grabbed his wrist and was pushing back with overwhelming strength.

"Whoah, Travis," the man on the ground said, "don't shoot, don't shoot."

Anac struggled, but he was pressed back bit by bit.

"Just relax, Anac, just relax. You didn't even unsheathe that thing, anyway."

He looked at the blade and realized that he had indeed left it in its pouch.

"We're not going to hurt you—either one of you," the one named Travis said, all the while keeping his drawn weapon pointed at Anac. "That's not what this is."

"He's right," the other said, Anac now getting off him and standing back up. "Just let us explain."

"I think you better," Reece said, breaking his long silence. "And since you ain't out to hurt us, and I tell you I ain't out to hurt no one who's just saved my life, how about putting that Taser away. We'll sit right here and listen, won't we, Anac?"

Travis hooked the weapon on his belt. Anac was breathing hard from the scuffle. He resumed his seat on the bumper, next to Reece, and waited.

"I'm Phillip," the cop said, up off the ground now. "This is Travis. You are—"

"Reece."

"Right. Reece. I'll talk to you first, because there's a choice you got to make before we can give Anac any real help. We are out to help him, so you know. Trust that."

"What choice?"

"There's no remaking it, now. So here it is—we give you $10,000 cash and you find your way back home and say nothing about any of this. You never met this guy. You never saw us. Your truck's at the scene, but you'll just have to report it stolen. We've got enough people on the force, we'll see that you don't get in trouble."

Reece looked down at his feet, then back up into Phillip's eyes. He acted, Anac thought, as if he had not heard. Then he spoke, quiet but firm, "What's the other choice?"

"We leave you off here with no money, and you do what-ever you want. Tell the whole story, tell the truth, whatever.

It's a complication for us—we'll have to disappear. But we can manage it."

"That's it?"

"That's it. $10,000 or nothing. I know you've seen enough movies to think we're supposed to threaten to shoot you or something. Nothing like that here. You'll just have to take our word that we are not crooked cops, not like you think. It's about him. Think of it as witness protection, or something."

"What's going to happen to him?" Reece asked.

"He'll be fine."

"Like the guy you killed in the car?"

"We saved your life."

No one spoke. Travis looked to the side, as if studying the tea-brown streams that rolled along the ditches. Phillip stood rubbing his elbow. The machine in the woods continued to groan and clank.

Reece broke the pause. "No deal," he said. "I'm not lying for you. That's out. Keep your money. But I ain't leaving him with you neither. I don't know what he's tied up in, but I trust him more'n I do y'all right now, so that's that. Leave us be and we'll get going."

"Not an option," said Phillip, "but I appreciate what you're saying. I do. How about this, you let us talk to your pal here—ten minutes will be enough, shoot, just five minutes—and he'll be telling you to take off. You don't want to lie for us, I appreciate that. I've been a cop for eleven years and I hate lying as much as anything. I appreciate that. Go tell your story—let folks try to make sense of it. But you can rest easy that Anac is going to be fine with us. We're his best bet right now." He looked to Anac. "Five minutes?"

"They know my son. Let me talk to them."

"Fine. Five minutes," Reece said.

Both cops walked up the road with Anac, who looked back several times as Reece, still leaning on the bumper, receded out of earshot. The five-minute meeting proved to only take two. He walked back to the vehicle, the cops trailing behind, and put his hand on Reece's shoulder. "It's alright," he said, "more than I can explain. You decide if you want to tell or not tell—I can't guide you on that—but you leave me with these guys. They're what I need."

Reece spit. He looked at the two cops. He looked into the trees, in the direction of the clanking. "I'm leaving," he said. "You might shoot me as I walk off, but I'm leaving. I don't trust any one of y'all. Something's up and you're in it and I don't care to know about it, but I do care to tell about it." He looked again toward the woods.

"You're safe. Go if you have to. I understand." With that, Phillip walked to the driver's side door, opened it, and pulled out a bottle of water. "Take this," he said, "and give us your cell phone. That'll at least buy us the time it takes you to walk over to that logging crew."

Reece didn't argue. He handed over his phone and looked at the three men around him. Then he took the water bottle and threw it hard onto the road. Its cap busted off and the clear water streamed onto the white dirt. He walked away, toward the woods.

"Reece," Anac said, but Reece did not slow. He hopped the ditch and worked his way into the thicket of the tree line. "Reece. Reece!" Anac called louder. But he was already disappearing into the greenery. "Reece! I just wanted to say, thank you."

"He can't understand," Phillip said, "and you can't expect him to." He picked up the bottle, still half filled with water, and handed it to Anac. "Ride in the back. We got to get going."

# Chapter 37

Anac sat alone in the back seat, perched in the middle so he could see the road ahead between the two deputies up front. He sipped the bottled water as they sped on. He was ready to talk, and to listen. But conversation had to wait on Travis to make calls. Phillip just stared out the window, smiling.

"Can you talk?" Travis asked into the radio.

"Yeah, go ahead," the high-pitched voice replied between bursts of static.

"Phillip saw his mark. We know it's Herson. What about the Tracc?"

Anac's chest tightened. This was the main item that sold him during the two-minute talk on the dirt road. They knew him, and they knew Sol—though not his location. They knew the agent, and they knew about Traccs. The deceased agent should have one on him, and Phillip and Travis claimed to be able to get it. Cementing the trust was that these guys were definitely not agents. Anac asked to see their chests and verified for himself that they had no BODs. That was enough. Their knowledge was still unaccountable, just like with Mr. Tifforp, but when this radio call ended, he was going to get some answers.

"No Tracc," the voice came back, along with breaks of loud scratches. "He would have had it on him, if he had it at all. Madison searched the bridge. She didn't find anything. Herson must have lost it in the water."

"10-4. What about the Stinger?"

"Yeah, non-Fam got to it before any of us could. It's in evidence. Why didn't you grab it? Didn't you look in his car?"

"There was no time to search. I messed up on that—it's unfortunate."

"Yeah. You didn't mess up on the other though. I mean, mission accomplished."

"Yes it is. Yes it is. Listen, some guy named Reece is going to be coming forward with what we did—ramming Herson and fleeing the scene and all. We'll just have to disappear and let them explain it how they will. Help us out all you can, but don't incriminate yourselves. Same with the Stinger. Just let them come up with their stories. Steal it if you can, but don't take big risks."

"10-4."

"You just tell the Family our work is done—that's all that matters now. Done. Finally done."

"Amen."

"Out."

"Out."


Travis began talking as soon as he signed off the radio. Anac had figured on asking his own questions, but the process was reversed.

"We need to know what happened on the bridge," he began, calmly. "Did you get the impression Herson had a Tracc?"

Anac felt easy with full disclosure. These guys somehow knew everything already. "I'm sure he did. He said he was about to kill me and send my corpse back. He asked me if Sol was with me. Then I think someone shot him. I dove in the river and Herson fell or jumped off the bridge not long after."

"That adds up. He must have dropped it when he got shot, or when he hit the water," Travis said. "He had a gunshot wound in his arm. Not enough to kill him, but sounds like it saved your life. If the Tracc's in the river it's probably— well, I mean, we might can get a dive team on it. It's not impossible."

"Oh."

Travis continued, "Why did he ask about Sol? He should have known all the details, right? The mission profile—"

"No, no," Phillip interrupted, "remember it says they had a ten-year window, but nothing was certain except Anac. Remember, because of—"

"Stop! Stop!" Anac shot out. "You two are going to start from the beginning. What do you know about Sol? How do you know all this? How do you know me? Who are you?"

The two deputies looked at one another. Travis shrugged his shoulders. Anac noticed for the first time how large his arms were. Neither man wore a hat, and both were dressed in identical black uniforms. Guns and other devices, one of which Reece had called a Taser, clung to their belts.

"We don't know where Sol is," Phillip said. "I'm sorry. We know, or we think we do, that he's somewhere near here, in time, I mean. He's certainly near here geographically. He landed the same place you did, just not the same time. There was a chance that he would be right next to you after the

Transport, but obviously no such luck, because you didn't see him."

"You're going too fast," Travis added. "Look. This is a long ride. We have plenty of time to talk. We have to get out of this state. We can explain. No sense in staying around if the Tracc is lost. Maybe we can search the river, but that's a long shot, and not with non-Fam cops crawling everywhere like now." The car was still bouncing down an unpaved road, though the dirt's color had changed from white to red. Travis was driving fast.

"No, no, no! I can't leave the state. I have to get to Darien."

"Darien? Why? We've got a lot of unwanted trouble around here. We need to make some distance."

"I have to go to Darien. There's a man there who knows about Sol. Have you heard of K. C. Sewell?"

"You know about Sewell?" Phillip asked, jerking his head around.

Anac nodded, "I mean, I've read his book. *The Rupture.* I don't know him, but he seems to know all about me."

"He would, if he were still around," Phillip looked ahead, out the front windshield. "I hate to tell you this. Sewell might could have helped when he wrote that book, but that was years ago, back in the eighties. He's gone now. Travis's dad looked for him soon after that book hit shelves, but there was no one to find. He was gone. Sewell only had forty days, just like you, you know. He would have had to leave on day thirty-nine. He did, we figure, and that was that." Phillip paused and looked out the side window, then went on in a lower voice, as if talking to himself, "Actually, Sewell's book, him knowing what he knew, helped hold our Family together. Faith was getting weak at that time, and Sewell was the ultimate reassurance."

This news of Sewell's absence hit Anac hard. The agent's Tracc was lost, Sol's whereabouts were a mystery, even to CHRON, and now the one follicle of hope, the man whose book indicated he knew something helpful, disappeared thirty years ago. What else was there? But *The Rupture* had called to him. It was plain. The author wanted to be sought out. Perhaps, though, the seeking had to be in the eighties. But that made no sense.

"I have to go to Darien," he said. "I have to go to Darien."

"But there's nothing there."

"I have to go to Darien."

"Anac."

"Give it up, Phillip. If it were your son, would you rest on someone else's word, without seeing for yourself? We'll take him, then we get out of Georgia. Alright with you, Anac? We'll show you what's in Darien." Travis picked up the radio, pressed a few buttons, then broke the static. "Mark, can you talk?"

"Go ahead."

"Family?"

"10-4. Go."

"Give them a lead to westward. Spread the dragnet away from Darien. Stall it that way as long as you can."

"I'll try. You need to kill some time, though. Hide a few hours at Creek's Mill, then go."

"Thanks. 10-76 Creek's Mill. Out."

"Out."

Putting down the radio, Travis looked at Phillip. "Alright," he said, "story time."

# Chapter 38

Grandpa never actually fished, but each week when his grandson came to visit, he insisted just the two of them head to the swamp pond while the rest stayed at the house tasting the desserts. The boy sat on the wooden bench in the faded red rowboat and stared at his bobber, smiling, waiting on Grandpa to do what Grandpa always did on these weekly trips.

"Well, Grandpa?"

"Oh I got it, I got it. I was just thinking about something. I brought a different book this time too, and I was just thinking if you were ready for it."

"Oh. What different book?"

"Well, let's just start with the fairy tales, and I'll see about that other after while." From his oversized tackle box—large because it had to hold the book of fairy tales, a volume that Grandpa always kept hidden there and never spoke about with anyone but his grandson—he removed a tattered brown book with a blank cover. "What'll it be today, Phil?"

"You know my favorite," Phillip said, still grinning and still staring at the unmoving orange bobber. Not a bite yet, but he didn't mind. The boat sat on the placid black water as if on a mirror, an inverted replica of the whole world descending below into the frozen reflection.

Grandpa began to read.

*One hundred years is a long time to wait, but that's just what Prince Phillip did. One hundred years is nothing at all, when at the end you get what you want. King Krazen had stolen the castle from Phillip's father by trickery and deceit, but a wizard foretold the day when Phillip would come out of hiding and have his revenge...*

The listening boy laid back on the boat's wooden bench and rested his head against a green cushion. He propped his feet on the gunwale, positioning the rod between his knees. He could not see the bobber from this position, but he was not worried. Actually, catching a fish in this pond was rare, and as usual, when Grandpa started reading and the stories started to take over, fishing no longer mattered. Soon enough, King Krazen was killed and Grandpa flipped over to another story.

*The old man lived in a hut by the great streams of Creideamh. Everyone in the village thought he was crazy, but he knew that when the time was right, they would see...*

Phillip checked his bait only once as the story rolled on, ended, and flowed into the next.

*The Dragon of Hilks would never have torched the town had the people kept their memories about them. That's the price of forgetting. It happened like this...*

After six stories, Grandpa closed the book and looked over the water and into the cypresses that formed its border. The boat tipped a little as Phillip sat up, sending a ripple that crept away into the trees. "You're stopping already?" he asked.

"No, I'm just thinking."

"About the other book?"

"Yes, about the other book."

"Where did you get it?"

"I've had it, since before you were born. I just haven't wanted to bring it out until you—until I felt you were ready."

"Ready?"

Grandpa opened his tackle box and swapped the fairy tales for another book, square and black. "You must never tell your parents."

"I know, I know. I've never told them about the fairy tales."

"Right, good. But especially they must never hear of this."

"I don't think they'd mind."

"Your father would," Grandpa said, looking straight at Phillip. "I read both these books to him as a child. He believed in them for a time, but when he moved off to school, eighteen years old, somehow he lost touch. He wouldn't like me reading these to you."

"Okay."

Grandpa opened the black book. He ran his hand across the first page, as if wiping dust away. He rubbed his chin. "Phil, do you like these fairy tales, I mean, really like them?"

"Of course. More than anything. Especially Prince Phillip."

"Have you ever dreamed about being Prince Phillip?"

"Well, yessir, I dream about being in lots of those stories, pretending."

"I used to do the same thing. I did. When I was your age and even older. I guess the truth is, I still do, even now. The stories give a certain purpose to my life, you know?" The old man smiled, rubbed his chin once more, and began to read.

*August 16, 1842. Parkson and Tagson—Declaration and Resolution: Revenge is all that matters. The story must be passed on until the year 2016 arrives. We will never personally see fulfillment of our revenge, but our posterity will, and that will be enough. The difficulty is in passing the tale down from generation to generation. To propagate a lasting lineage, we must marry, and we cannot expect our wives to believe. The faith must go straight to our offspring, cloaked well enough to pass unnoticed, but truthful enough to be effective. Thus, we have resolved to compose a book of fairy tales—a type of literature popular in this century. It seems, for these people, nearly anything is permissible so long as it is labeled a fairy tale. We will pass on the core ideas to our children through these. Though at some point, at the key moment, the mask will be removed and the offspring will be told—the stories are real, and the time is indeed coming...*

Phillip didn't check his bait again the rest of the day.

# Chapter 39

DAY 3

*That ride with Phillip and Travis was surreal. They talked nonstop during our layover at Creek's Mill, then on and on as the miles rolled away toward Darien. I heard all about the origin of the Family. What a mighty chain of events had conspired to intersect their paths with mine after so many years! But they had their revenge. They killed the one who betrayed them, and in the process they saved my life. I mostly sat silent, absorbing. The saddest part of the tale to me, naturally, was how Herson stole Parkson's and Tagson's Traccs before he made his escape. How I'd love to have those, but they were gone. Herson had left the marooned agents their Stingers, which they subsequently destroyed as they tried to assimilate to the 19^{th} century—to build a life there and, what mattered most, to start families. No children equaled no revenge.*

*I asked them why the fairy tales. Why not just go straight to the black book? They gave two reasons. 1) When a descendant of Parkson or Tagson married, you couldn't expect the spouse to understand, so the offspring had to be taught in secret. 2) The gravity and peculiarity of the truth was hard even for children to accept,* and the Family found it more effective to lay some prerequisite groundwork; fictional, yes, but built on the right foundation.

I asked if it always worked, this fairy tale then black book method. They said no. Apparently it had found closed ears as often as open ones. Enough believers remained to keep the truth alive until 2016, as I had seen play out before my eyes, but there were dry patches—a bad one in the1970s. For a while, it seemed no one would be left to receive Herson when he arrived. Phillip's dad, for instance, abandoned the faith, which is why Phillip had to get it from Grandpa on those weekly fishing trips.

Still, so they told me, the Family is fairly extensive. Spotting a possible connection, I asked if they knew anyone named Tifforp. Was he part of the Family? They said they'd never heard that name. I told them about my experience in Westend, and showed them the lure and the slip of paper inside—still in my pocket, the paper kept dry by its protective capsule. They looked over the number, punched it into their phones, and explained that ISBNs refer to specific books. My number, though, turned up no matches— something called the "internet" told them this, with certainty, they said. I asked if it might connect to their book of fairy tales, or maybe the black book. They said no, neither of those had an ISBN because neither had ever been published.

Then the sign: WELCOME TO DARIEN. I grew silent. Travis reminded me what they had told me before. "Don't get your hopes up, Anac," he said. "We told you, Sewell is long gone."

# Chapter 40

As they crossed the bridge into Darien, the surrounding landscape was unlike anything he had yet seen in the 21st century. The sun was lowering to westward, and with golden spears it reached over a flat field of tall grass interwoven with water canals in a complicated pattern. The bridge passed a wide river, and far off to both sides Anac could see tiny rivulets reaching out from the main channel, disappearing into the thick grasslands. A smell hung thick in the air.

The bridge began its gentle descent as he took in the town. Large boats lined the edge of the river. Two of them had bright lights bathing their decks and spilling over to the water. The buildings along the shore were a mixture of tall and short, of pristine and dilapidated. None resembled the typical house styles he had noticed in Corston. Houses like Samuel's and Scott's were one thing—these were another. Some were huge. Several appeared to be built out of a sort of stone. And their roofs were as often flat as peaked.

"Does Sewell live in one of these?"

"You mean *did*, and no, he didn't. He lived down the river just a short piece."

The bridge transitioned smoothly to the mainland, and Travis took a road to the right. Anac studied a line of block buildings. He was coming to realize that his hope, swelled with time and focus, had taken in his mind the shape of a town as much as a person. Sewell of Darien was his link to Sol, his only viable chance, and not just the man but also the town had become his obsession. And now, here it was. Buildings and boats and, he hated to admit, nothing helpful. Nothing at all without the presence of the one man who might know something. His being here meant everything—and these cops said he was gone.

"There," Phillip announced.

Anac's heart tightened. He felt short of breath, which made him think of Sol, coping alone somewhere without his breathing medicine, without Daddy.

He looked through the back seat's cage and out the front windshield to the house. It was gray and square and tall, oddly tall compared to other houses—out of proportion, too narrow for its height. Travis turned into the drive and parked on a gravel patch flanked all around with high grass. Thick weeds grew along the walls of the house, and though the sun had set into evening, not a light shined through any window. All was black. They stepped out of the car. He then noticed one light at the highest peak of the house shining dimly out of a roundish room walled with glass on all sides.

"Easy enough house to remember," Phillip said. "Sewell, or whoever it was, built it to look like a lighthouse."

"Do we knock?" Anac asked.

"Sure."

The three walked to the door, led by the headlights from the still-running car, and Travis gave a hard pound with the pad of his fist. He also pressed a button to the left of the door.

Nothing happened. Anac's heart raced. A strange intermingling of hope-found and all-hope-lost made his head watery, but there was nothing to be done. The man who wrote *The Rupture* was either here or not here. Travis pounded again.

They waited.

"Stay by the door," Travis said. "We'll do a walk around." And as if rehearsed, the two cops pulled slender flashlights from their shirt pockets and walked away in opposite directions, obviously to search the backside of the house. Anac stood there, never wanting a door to open so badly as he did right now. The darkness was deepening, and the night sounds swelled as he stared at the door, fighting an urge to scream at it, yank on it, kick it down. Instead, he just stood at the door and knocked. No sound came from within, and no light flicked on to shine its hope through the window. Then the hand came over his mouth.

A sharp, whispered voice. "Don't scream."

He reacted unthinkingly, clawing at the large hand that had cut off his air. But just as immediately he saw a familiar face and heard a familiar voice.

"Anac, it's us, it's us, don't scream. Let's go." It was Samuel. "No time. Now. Let's go," he spat out in whispered firmness. "That shed across the street," and he pointed as they began to move. The other man released him.

"But what—"

"Not now," the large stranger whispered.

Knowing only that he trusted Samuel, he obeyed, and the three ran past the cop car and toward the road. They were in the middle of the street when the shouts came.

"Hey! Hey! Stop!" It was Travis.

"Go!" Samuel said, and turned not toward the shed but up the road. Anac did not understand, but he followed, and the three were running full sprint now, though his foot throbbed with this new exertion, allowing him only a painful hobble. Samuel and the other man—whom Anac suddenly remembered as the fellow from that strobing building the night of the Dogs—did not rush out ahead, but kept pace with Anac, apparently to aid him.

"Go, go, go, go," Samuel fired out. "My truck's by the landing."

"Hey! Anac!" came calls from behind.

"Don't stop," Samuel said, but the bouncing beams of the flashlights and the pounding of boots were getting closer. Soon the distance was nearly nothing. "Keep going, Anac," Samuel said, and then he and the other man stopped and faced the cops.

Anac did not understand, nor did he keep going. Friends from one end of his sojourn seemed at odds with friends from the other end. A scuffle broke out, the purpose of which he could not follow, but he joined in, trying mostly to protect, to break up. "Stop it! Stop it! What is this? What are you doing?"

"A. J., get him out of here!" Samuel grunted, deadlocked with Travis, who in the next moment rolled them both to the ground.

A. J.'s strong arm grabbed Anac's shoulder and pushed him—catapulted him—out of the fight, while his other arm pressed Phillip away. Anac jumped right back into the fray to try and make peace. He saw that Samuel and Travis were in a scraping roll on the ground, shirts ripping and skin tearing. He also saw that Phillip was reaching for his Taser.

"No! No! No!" he cried, rushing back in. "These are my friends! Stop it!"

In the darkness and the shuffling and the shouting, as Phillip was just getting his weapon off his belt and Anac was just getting in his face to stop him, a sixth man rushed out of the darkness and locked around Phillip's arm, using his little weight—he was a thin person—to try and pull the arm down to get the Taser pointed toward the ground. The delay was brief, but proved enough to get A. J. behind them both. He swallowed the two in a wide bear hug. Anac reached for the Taser, hardly knowing what to do. Travis, who had untangled from Samuel, crawled back on all fours then popped up to his feet and pulled out a weapon from his belt. Gleaming silver—not a Taser.

"Don't shoot! Don't shoot!" the thin stranger called, locked in place by A. J.'s arms. All stood frozen now under the aim of Travis's gun.

"Everyone please just stop," Anac pleaded. "Please, Samuel, everyone, these guys are my friends. They saved my life. They brought me to find Sewell!"

"Good," the stranger said, "and I'm Sewell."

# Chapter 41

*Sol, I got a tattoo today. A. J. had one on his arm. That's what gave me the idea. Actually, part of mine, the image, is just like his, though mine is larger, and it's on my chest rather than my arm. Samuel is here again. He took me to get it. Some shop in the next town, Brunswick. I wanted names, maybe even the whole story, a short version, inked on my chest. But Birshop said before he left that I could get neither names nor story. He firmly said so. He said details like that could do a great deal of harm. The Tysar Effect. I obeyed. But I doubt the ink I did get will do any great deal of good.*

*I miss you so much. Is your breathing giving you trouble? Your breathing. Isn't that proof enough? Can't you remember? Can't we remember?*

# Chapter 42

The five dirtied and bruised men sat around a large, purple rug in a high upper room, only one level below the glass peak that sent out the light from the faux lighthouse. The chairs around the room were cloth, layered with dust. Sewell was preparing tea. He insisted on this before he would give his explanation. As he clinked with cups at a desk in the far corner of the room, Anac took the silent moment to lean over toward Samuel. "Why is he here?" he asked, nodding to A. J., who was sitting to Samuel's right. "And why are *you* here?"

"He came because I asked him to. We went to high school together, years ago—been friends ever since. Brothers, really. I came for you. Night before last, I tossed the Tracker on a semi. Then I went back to the camp house, but the agent and Sewell's book were gone. I figured he was onto you and Darien. We saw yesterday on the news about the shooting at the bridge, the dead sheriff and the two men who ended up in the river, the strange wounds on the deputy's body. I knew it involved you, and I did what I had half thought to do anyway, which was chase you down. Why did you run away?"

"I, uh—but how did you know I'd be here?"

"I didn't know anything, but since I had no leads, and couldn't search the river any more than the cops were doing, I figured I could only head where I knew you were heading and hope we both made it. Then I heard the report on the news," here Samuel spoke louder and shot a glare at Phillip and Travis who sat across the circle, "about these two rogue cops who had murdered a man and kidnapped two others, one of whom had escaped. And about the strange weapon found on the scene, and all I knew was you were in some kind of trouble, and I needed to get you away from them if I could."

"But they—"

"Not now," the man called Sewell said as he handed out small white cups. "You'll have to explain the Family later. There'll be time. Hey," and he looked toward A. J., "you're of The Order, I see."

"What?" A. J. asked.

"That tattoo on your arm."

Everyone looked at the black ink on the brown bicep.

Travis spoke up, "But Dad said you were gone, that you must have left before your fortieth day, decades ago."

Sewell sat down in a narrow chair by the rug's corner. He sipped his tea and placed it on a small side table. "I am not K. C. Sewell," he said.

Anac jolted up, "What?"

"Sit down, sit down. It's alright," the man said. "Sewell is human just like you, and not an agent either. Anyone without a Gor-Implant will only have a 39-day window within which to work. Your dad was right," he looked at Travis, "the first Sewell left on his 39th day. But if we'd wanted interaction with the Family, we'd have let your dad find us."

"But you said—"

"My name is Birshop. But I work in the name of Sewell,

as did my predecessor and his predecessor before him, all the way back to the original that your father looked for in the eighties."

"So who *are* you?" Samuel asked.

"I am a shiftworker, a 39-day replacement of a 39-day replacement, but authorized to function in the name of Sewell, who actually wrote *The Rupture*, which is our draw, our one draw."

"Draw of what?" Anac asked. No one was interested in the tea except Sewell—that is, Birshop—who agonized Anac with slow sipping pauses before each answer.

"Of you, of Sol, of anyone temporally displaced. CHRON really has no true idea of what they're doing. Temporal Transport is a great evil, and The Order works against it every day. CHRON always transports to the future, and therefore, our rescue missions are always to the future. Except for you and Sol. This case is unique."

"Sol is here, then? I mean, in the past?" Anac asked.

Birshop's explanation was accompanied by a dull internal hum, a growing, pulsing throb behind Anac's ears. This was too much, too real, too near. And, worst of all, too far, for through the hum he heard Birshop explain at length about Sol being as yet unfound, and about Sewell publishing in the eighties because that was The Order's best estimate as to when Sol and Anac might have landed, somewhere in the half century after 1987. Sol had still not come. He might be anywhere—perhaps ten years ahead, perhaps ten years past. In that case he must have missed finding *The Rupture*, which, Birshop explained, is all too common on rescue missions.

Of course, they had been doing more proactive searching as well. Every day of every year since 1987, the shiftworkers had looked for reports of strange sightings, of unidentified persons found in the area. They had pictures of Sol and Anac in their mission profile. But, as Birshop explained, Temporal Transportees often have a natural inclination to stay unnoticed. Though it seems they would be an intrusive presence, they often are successful at blending in. Birshop firmly asserted that time and trial have shown the book-draw method to be the most effective. Anac could hardly refute it, for here he was.

"There's a catch, though," Birshop said, for once not caring about his tea. "This mission is, well, I hardly know how to say this—it is just for one of you. You showed up first, so it's you we've saved. You see, The Order is spread terribly thin, with outposts all through the next millennium. It's only by the barest chance that we had any Traccs at all for this mission, and they're not even the typical Auto-Traccs. They are two prototype devices The Order managed to take from a CHRON research facility. Unlike Auto-Traccs, these can only carry one person. The point is, Anac, there's one to get me back to my family and one to get you back to your wife."

The throb in his head had swollen to its maximum by this point, and then it snapped off with a sharp ping. He could hardly believe what he was hearing. This was his hope and his help, and what help was it if it meant he could be saved only while his son had to perish?

"And this is no time to be noble," Birshop added. "Maybe if we kept the shiftwork up Sol would eventually show, but just as likely he has already been missed, in which case he's passed his forty days and will never be drawn by *The Rupture* now. Plus—you might not know this—Traccs function by a sort of fundamental dance between the human mind, specifically memory, and what we call the Core Power. Those fool CHRONs call it the Void Power, which to them is just a temporary term given to what they actually believe is nothing at all and will one day be debunked altogether. They can't un-name it yet, though, because they keep seeing and counting on its effects. But they are convinced it is just a void, an absence, a vacuum, which is why they will never understand what it is they're actually doing.

"It's the so-called Void Power that made them push for the BODs in the first place. Didn't you ever wonder why they mandated those so vehemently? Why the implant was right above the heart? Hikerson said it all along. But that's not the point right now. You want your son home, I know. You would give up your Tracc to leave it for him, I know. But it's futile, and I'm sorry. Once Sol's memory is wiped, which quite possibly it already has been, the Tracc would do him no good. Traccs require the user to have a foundational belief that time jumps are possible. Only within that post-Fracture mental framework can a Tracc do its work. I can't imagine bringing a wiped mind in this century to a place where it could view time from the 29th-century paradigm."

Anac sat still, staring at the fibers of the rug beneath his feet, hating that rug and this house and this news and this man—this help that was no help.

Phillip broke the silence, "Do you mean it is possible, plausible, even without a full memory?"

"Theoretically, yes. Ever read *The Dark Tower*? That's about as close as—"

"You said The Order is trying to save the displaced," Anac interrupted, "but what good is it if you leave a father without his son? How dare you put me in a place like this, with this choice?"

"There is no choice. Sewell's rules. Mission parameters. The first one of you to show means the end of the shiftwork in this time. If you refuse to come back with me—and I won't make you go—Sewell won't allow us to return to the past. You'll be here alone, and soon with no memory of your son. Even if he ever were to show, you wouldn't know him. Home we go. Sewell's orders."

"Sewell's orders! What good is Sewell then?" He was standing before he realized it, pacing up and down the rug in his rant. "Maybe you idiots should quit seeking the displaced and just stop CHRON from displacing at all! None of you smart enough to ever think of that? Especially since you only find us to tell us you can't really do much other than force a father to leave his son in exile."

"I understand, Anac, and I'm sorry," Birshop said calmly. "We really did try. Truly. But we were delayed the day of your Transport and got in too late."

"Too late? Got in where?"

"Maybe I should show you Sewell." Birshop produced from his pocket a device that Anac had not seen since his departure, a 29th-century VIC. He rose and walked across the rug, holding the display for Anac to see. There it was, Sewell's image. Anac recognized him immediately. He was the bearded man from the Transport Room—the intruder who blew the bomb.

# Chapter 43

The night carried a cold breeze.

"I'm so sorry," Samuel said. He leaned his forearms on the rail next to Anac and stared silently over the marsh. They stood on the catwalk around the house's peak.

"You know I can't go."

"I sure figured it," Samuel spit over the side, then rapped his knuckles on the iron banister. "But it does seem like... I mean, look, one death doesn't merit another. It's not your fault what they did to you and your boy, but they did do it, and if only one of you can make it back, well, that's better than both being lost. Think about your wife."

"She's all I ever think about. Her and Sol. That's all. It's a strange thing being a husband and dad. You don't know that yet, but it is."

"Yeah."

"I can't go."

A door creaked behind them. They turned, and Birshop was there. He didn't say anything, but held out with both hands a small brown box, lidless and lined with a green padding. Anac saw them, two Traccs. A horn sounded somewhere out in the marsh—deep and mellow. Anac was crying now. No heaves or gasps, but the steady, quiet flow of brokenness. He reached into the box and pulled out one of the devices. "Are they both the same?" he asked.

"Yes, both Free-Traccs. The prototypes. One for each of us."

"One for me."

"Yes."

He studied it closely. He looked at the corner where his eye would go to activate the time jump.

"We can get you home tonight if you like," Birshop said softly.

Anac glared back at him, wiped his eyes with his sleeve, then crammed the Tracc into his pocket. "I'm only going to say this once, and then I don't want either of you to bring it up. This Tracc is for Sol. Don't you ever tempt me with it again. You hear that? Never again. I'll get Sol to remember. I'll give him enough connection. I'll get this to him."

"But how—"

"Never again!"

And no one said another word for some time. Samuel resumed his position at the rail. Anac joined him. Birshop did too. The deep horn sounded once more, and a spotlight swept left and right from a large boat motoring up the river.

"Shrimpers," Samuel said. "And fishermen in that smaller boat. See it there? The one anchored on the far side."

"Fishermen."

"Yup. For catfish, I guess, or really I don't know."

This reminded Anac of something, and he turned to Birshop. "Have you ever heard of a man named Tifforp?"

"Tifforp? No."

"He gave me this," and he pulled out the lure, then popped it open and handed the paper to Birshop. "Phillip and Travis said it's a number for a book, but they checked it and couldn't find a match."

"You think he gave it to you on purpose?"

"More than that—he knew who I was. Knew about Herson. He even helped me get away on the train."

Birshop studied the number, then handed it back. "I see. In that case, you need to keep it. The paper I mean. Keep it safe."

"What is it?" Samuel asked.

"There are those who cross our paths from time to time—the paths of the shiftworkers, I mean. This is the first experience I've had with it personally, but it's part of our training. Helpers. Unsolicited and unexplained assistance. Actually, The Order doesn't know much about them. We just call them prophets. It's believed they are somehow outside of time altogether. Whoever or whatever they are, they always know more than we do, and their help is always to be heeded."

Anac replaced the paper in the lure and put it in the same pocket as the Tracc. He stood, thinking. "How long do you have left?" he asked Birshop.

"Eight more days."

"Eight more."

"Yeah," Birshop pulled up off the rail and stood straight. "If you're set on staying, we might as well make a plan. For one thing, I've got a book I'll leave you. *First Principles.* It's a CHRON Publication. You should destroy it before your time runs out. It might help you some. I don't know. And how will you draw Sol, really, Anac?"

"The same way Sewell drew me. I'll write. I'll publish. I'll cast the net wide and hope he finds it, hope he remembers."

"I'll pray he does," said Samuel. "It's a brave thing you're doing, taking such long odds for your boy. Really it is. I hope it leads him to you."

"Not to me," he said. "I won't remember—" here he choked hard on his tears. "I won't even know him. The clues are going to have to lead him to someone who will." He yanked his sleeve across his cheek. "To you, Samuel. You're the one. I need you to do this for me. This one thing."

Hours later, when everyone else in the house was asleep, Anac rose and climbed back to the glass crown atop the lighthouse. He did not open the door onto the walkway. Instead he sat on the interior floor with his back against the glass. He flipped the switch over his head that turned on the light in the center of the room. With a steady hand, he uncapped a borrowed pen and brought it to a borrowed book—gifts from Birshop. His tears were over, evaporated by the clear salt winds of purpose. He had entered a mode of dry eyes, and he would see to it they stayed that way. His self was dead now. From here to the end, all that mattered was the work, the words, the grasping link to his son. Tunneled, focused, unwavering desire. He took a deep breath and scratched the pen across the first page: *DAY 36.*

# Chapter 44

Now to pull back the curtain. Anac—though he would not recognize that name now—is living near Phillip in southern Florida. They got him set up with a new life, a job in a bookstore. And they stay involved, the Family, lots of them, more than just Phillip and Travis. I guess they needed a new purpose, having fully finished their century-old mission. From the updates they've given me, it's been a strong success. To get his new life started, to give it context, they treated him as an amnesiac, the victim of a hit and run, so they told him. My task, sadly, proved less successful.

I went back to Darien, as instructed, on the thirty-ninth day. I met Anac at the lighthouse, where he'd stayed the whole time, writing furiously. That evening he had me drive him to a tattoo parlor. Then we sat up the rest of the night atop Sewell's lighthouse. Birshop was long gone. Phillip and Travis were coming in the morning. We talked all night, me mostly listening as he went on and on about Sol and Rachel. He wrote one more entry just before sunrise, then gave me the journal, entrusting me with publication.

That's what I mean about being less successful. I soon learned how hard such a thing is. Of course, there was self-publishing. I had some money for that, but the whole point was for the book to land in the unsuspecting hands of an amnesiac Sol. Popularity was our weapon. Marketing.

Miranda, my wife, read it all through and told me her opinion. "This will never make it," she said. "I think you'll have to try some changes."

I had my ethical concerns with this, but weighed against the fear that each passing day we might be missing our target, I soon relented.

But passing days turned out to be unavoidable. I wrote, reworked, submitted. I solicited advice from some colleagues at the high school where I teach. I reworked again. All to no avail. My naivety was laughable. No publisher would touch it. They said "Too long"; they said "Too slow"; they said "Too archaic"; they said, most often, nothing.

My resolve grew in proportion to my frustration, and the days and months clicked by. After two years, I knew I needed a fresh approach. I enrolled in a creative writing program at a college in the mountains of north Georgia. For three years, even amid the pandemic, I studied, rewrote, and rethought. It was there I fully realized how to capitalize on what I had been naturally doing all along. Obviously, anytime I shared Anac's journal with anyone, it was taken as fiction. That was the only way I could present it without seeming crazy. During my three years in the program, I realized that fully accepting the wide parameters fiction offers was the only way. I eventually repackaged the journal as a science fiction adventure, sprinkling throughout short excerpts from the original journal and dramatizing the rest—as you've seen.

Even amid the fiction, I strove to maintain fidelity to

the events as Anac recorded them. My main task was not altering, but deleting. So much left out! For instance, Anac's lengthy explanation of the Fracture of the 2300s. And all that business about the earthquakes. Also, the several excerpts he copied from the volume entitled *First Principles*—a book he destroyed.

Then there was the language. Anac's journal was in the vernacular of the 29th century, which, though readable, was better translated. The *Riddley Walker* approach didn't work in this case.

Similarly, I cut the endless—though never debilitating—complications his dialect caused during his 2016 sojourn, and I greatly downplayed the difficulty he had in learning 21st-century speech. VIC, for instance, stands for "Wrist Inter-Communicator," but I left the gap between "V" and "W" unbridged in the narrative—their word for "wrist" starts with "V." You can imagine the liberties I had to take with idioms.

As to dates, I converted all to the Gregorian calendar. The CHRON calendar, while still measuring in years ("yeegs" in their language), uses the Fracture as a starting point. Anac was arrested as an Under in the year 477 and landed amid my Civil War reenactment in -376 (our 2016). Minutes, seconds, feet, inches—all foreign terms to a 29th-century resident—Anac did the work of converting, along with tedious explanations. In the novel, I simply converted without apology. And on the subject of trimming, I heavily downplayed Anac's bigotry about height. Its degree would shock a 2020s reader, and to construct the deep-seated strength of Anac's preference for the tall—and his complete (and admirable) ob-liviousness to skin color—would have bogged the narrative.

But it was fascinating, and, I'm sure, a large part of why he trusted me as readily as he did. I'm six foot two. As to why I trusted him as readily as I did, well, you'd have to believe in prayer to get that. Try Acts 9:10. My novel may be serving a larger purpose than just getting Sol home.

Of course, for the scenes where Herson is alone, I relied on conjecture. But based on Anac's account in the journal and personal testimonies from the Family, the story is close enough to fact, where it can be. There were other conjectural liberties here and there. The business of the Lort, for instance. Anac never gave me a clear picture on this topic. His journal was strangely laconic on the issue. At first I speculated that Lorts must be akin to some of our 21st-century drugs, opi-oids and so forth. Somehow, though, this hypothesis never satisfied me, and it's too late to talk to him about it now. So I did the best I could, fudging where I had to, navigating the delicate balance between staying faithful to the original facts and crafting a marketable narrative.

Then, one day, it happened. An email from a press, and not a small one. The goal was finally attained. But that's all history. What matters now is that it's out there—on the shelves, on the internet. I have several copies at my house and several more in my classroom. Every teacher friend I know across the state I try to get to teach it. Sol might be school age, after all, depending on when he landed. I've turned into a promoter, feeling it's the only thing left I can do for Anac—my friend who lives only a few hours from me yet has no idea who I am, who he is, or what this is about.

Birshop told us about how real a problem The Order has with shiftworkers forgetting their purpose while at a post. Not a forty-day memory wipe, but rather a drifting from why they are there. They forget what they are about. Birshop said they just seem to fall in love with the time of their outpost and never come back. I have vowed that nothing like this will happen to me. If by some thousandth chance Sol finds the book, and by a thousandth more it actually draws him, I'll be here to receive. I'll have the Tracc ready. It's ready now, waiting for Sol, wherever he is.

# Chapter 45

## ADDENDUM TO THE 2ND EDITION

The roof shadowed the noon sun and provided a moment of relief from the sticky Georgia heat. Above the house, the large limbs of an oak tree canopied the front yard and the porch. The man took in the surroundings and again checked the address on his index card. Seeing no bell, he knocked three times on the screen door. It clattered against the frame. He waited, staring at a fish-shaped decoration nailed to the white wood wall. No answer. He pulled and found the screen unlatched, so he knocked on the door itself and got a more satisfying sound. Hearing footsteps within, he closed the screen and stood waiting. *They'll think I'm crazy*, he thought to himself. He crossed his hands in front of him awkwardly, stuffed the index card in his pocket, and wiped the sweat from his forehead.

The door opened, revealing a tall man dressed in khakis and a blue button-up shirt, the sleeves rolled to the elbow, a pen in his front pocket. "Good afternoon," the tall man said, a large smile spreading wide on his face.

"Good afternoon," the man on the porch replied. "I, um, well... Are you Samuel Yawn?" he stammered.

"Yes. Yes. That's me."

"I'm Kevin Dykes," he said, and then, reaching down, he picked up a paperback book and held it square in front of the door. He gathered his nerve for this long-rehearsed question. "Did you write this book?"

"Yes, yes."

"I'm sorry to bother you, really, but I have something I want to ask you."

"Oh, sure, happy to. Come in please." Mr. Yawn pushed on the screen, flipping it wide open, and Kevin walked in. The author seemed inviting, obviously happy to have a visitor. His smile had steadily grown since he answered the knock. Kevin closed the door behind him to trap in the air conditioning that filled the room, billowing from a window-unit over the sofa.

"Sit there, please," Mr. Yawn instructed, himself taking a thin yellow chair under a lamp. "I'm happy for questions. Can I ask you something first?"

"Yes, of course." Kevin had not expected this.

"You've read it. Have you felt a strange connection to it? Something deep inside?"

Kevin was struck hard. "Mr. Yawn, I have read your book exactly eighty-six times. I can't explain that. Eighty-six. I normally read a book once, twice at the most. But I've never felt about a book as I do of yours. Do you get this all the time?"

"No. Well, only once before."

"I have to know. I don't know why it bothers me so bad.

I have to know. Did the boy in the story, Sol, did the journal draw him in?"

"What do you mean? Like, if I wrote a sequel?"

"Um. Yes, of course, right—what would happen if you wrote one?"

"The journal drew him. He came."

"He got the Free-Tracc?"

"Yes."

"And Anac?"

"He lived out his days not knowing the hero he was." Then, inexplicably, a tear rolled down Mr. Yawn's cheek. He wiped it quickly with an open hand.

"I've bothered you. I'm sorry. I'll go."

"No, no. It's nothing. It's not you. What else?"

"So, Anac lived out—I mean, would live out—his days that way, because there were no more Traccs, right?"

"There was one more."

"How?"

"Don't you remember what the cops said, about the dive team?"

"They found it?" Kevin was struggling to distinguish if he was picking an author's mind about a fiction, or asking a real man a real question. And more tears streaked Mr. Yawn's cheeks, which wasn't helping. Kevin rubbed his chest as he wavered on a decision. The last thing he wanted was to be thought crazy. He knew all too much about that. But the really last thing he wanted was to leave here without a question answered.

"Samuel."

"Yes."

"I want to ask you something. And please, just—"

"It's alright. Go ahead."

"Well, I want to know—" and here Kevin pulled down his shirt collar, revealing the upper part of his chest, showing his ink. "I want to know why this is on my chest? And somehow I feel like—I know this sounds crazy—I feel like you can help me."

Samuel did not reply for some time. He stared at the markings. The tattoo was a fish outline, and inside its border was an ISBN.

"That number is for your book."

"I know," Samuel replied. He wiped his face several times and stared at the rug, deep in thought. Eventually, without a word, he rose and left the room. Kevin sat alone, lost. Then footsteps returned up the hall, and Samuel entered, this time holding a small black device. He handed it to Kevin.

"Is this a—"

"It's yours if you want it," Samuel said.

Kevin stared at the item.

"It's all yours." A breath. "Anac."

He looked at Samuel, startled, shaken, afraid. He touched his hand to his chest, feeling the fish and the number printed over his heart. He leaned forward wordlessly, dazed, bringing his eye to the hole in the corner of the black device that now seemed strangely familiar. Then all turned to water and washed him away, home.

# AUTHOR'S NOTE:
# SPREAD THE WORD!

Wes would greatly appreciate you leaving an honest review on Amazon.com (or Goodreads, or wherever books are rated). Also, if you loved *Reaching Sol*, please share on your social media pages. Find more at wesyoungwriter.com.

# ACKNOWLEDGMENTS

Grateful thanks to Ron Butchart, who taught me how to learn. To Dallas Cowne, who taught me how to teach. To John Williams (*Lake Moon*, 2002), who taught me how to write; I would trade all my books if I could craft prose like he does. To Gray Stewart (*Haylow*, 2016), who taught me how to rewrite; I've never met anyone with such an understanding of narratives. Thanks also to Luke Madden for his close reading and valuable input on this manuscript. To Penny and Russell Spivey for their generous copyediting comments, and for the idea of including a glossary. To Emily-Lisa Thornton for her proofreading. To Erin NeSmith, Emily Wiegert, and Lainie Partain (see copyright page). To Daniel O'Connor, Attorney at Law, for contractual assistance. To the Reinhardt staff—Donna, Bill, and the rest—for their wonderful program. To the Etowah Valley MFA class of 2020. To the Bleckley County High School Language Department, all great encouragers. To Bleckley County Schools as a whole, the best little school system in the state. To my wonderful church family at Limestone Baptist Church, Cochran. To the mentors I never met: George MacDonald, G. K. Chesterton, and especially C. S. Lewis (*Reaching Sol* is my thank-you letter to him).

To Mom and Dad for, let's be honest, everything; I was not yet ten years old when I got my first rejection letter from a publisher, but neither that nor anything else in life has been too much to take, because my parents have always had my back. To Nikki and Mariah, whose playful noises are the background of all my writing. Most of all, to Robin, for her endless love and support—there is none like her, and I would be lost, lost, lost without this amazing woman.

To all the others who deserve thanks—too many to list here. Finally, all glory to God the Father and His Son Jesus Christ, who are my hope.

# ABOUT THE AUTHOR

Wes Young teaches literature at Bleckley County High School where he serves as chair of the Language Department. He is a three-time recipient of the Teacher of the Year award and was also recognized as the 2021 District Teacher of the Year. He preaches (pulpit supply) in the middle Georgia area and was ordained to the Gospel ministry in 2013. He is a graduate of Bleckley County High School (2005), the University of Georgia (2009), and the Etowah Valley MFA at Reinhardt University (2020). As a lifelong middle Georgia resident, he knows the South as it really is, and seeks to portray the place and people authentically in his writings. He is a passionate advocate for adoption and foster care and hopes all children will be fortunate enough to find good families. He is a member of Limestone Baptist Church, Cochran, and lives nearby on two acres inhabited by a dog, a rabbit, two cats, and several goats. He shares these crazy acres with his beautiful wife (who brings life to life) and his two amazing daughters (who make each day interesting). Find out more at wesyoungwriter.com.